FORTY, FABULOUS AND...FAE?

MIDLIFE MAYHEM BOOK ONE

MELINDA CHASE

D1446085

Edited by Chris T. Edits

MIDLIFE MAYHEM BOOK ONE

No one expects their happily-ever-after to end at forty—but here I am one Prince Charming short of a fairytale.

Living back at Mom's place with her and Gram is not how this ex district attorney intended to start the next chapter of her life, but I shouldn't be surprised it's where I ended up.

You see, my family is cursed. *Literally.*

At least that's what both Gram and Mom claim. I've never given much thought to their ridiculous superstitions, but when three local patrons from my mom's occult shop end up dead, even I'm a bit unnerved.

So, I decide to dive right into the crazy headfirst. And what I thought would be the end of my journey...may only be the beginning.

1

"TAKE THE STUPID SHOES!" I screeched, while simultaneously launching my hardly worn pair of Louboutin's straight at my husband's head.

Ex-husband. I needed to start remembering that tiny, yet very significant detail.

To my absolute horror, Kenneth managed to duck, and narrowly avoided getting stabbed in the eye with the very sharp, stupidly irresponsible, and impossible to wear heel.

If only I had learned to throw when I was a child. Maybe that moment would have turned out differently.

But I guess I should back up a little bit.

My name is Shannon McCarthy. A boring name for a boring woman. And even more boring? Here I am, barely forty, the victim of a male midlife crisis, newly divorced, and forced to move back home to Portland, Oregon. Well, not forced. But right now, Portland seemed like a much better choice than Boston, where news of my husband's affair still littered the front pages of our local newspaper.

Who would have thought my life would turn out like this?

Not me, that's for damn sure. When I married Kenneth, with his smooth tan skin and devilish good looks, I really thought that was it for me. This was the guy I'd spend the rest of my life with. We'd have two very high profile careers, me as a D.A., and him as a judge, live in a big fancy house with a purebred Golden Retriever who listened to our every single command, and drive shiny new sports cars, like a Lamborghini, to and from our high-paying jobs every day. It was the life every single Boston girl dreams of.

And apparently, it was a life I no longer got to have. Not since Kenneth decided his pretty, young clerk was the place he should stick his junk, instead of being a respectable man and coming home to his wife.

So, here we were. I was in the middle of packing up the home we'd bought ten years ago, the one we were supposed to grow old in, while Kenneth sat on his butt and complained about every single thing I tried to box up. Anything he had bought me during the fifteen years we'd been married was apparently just a reminder of how much he had "given" me over the years.

As if I hadn't given him anything, too. I was the one who'd worked my tiny little butt off to put him through law school when I was on a public defender's salary, saving and pinching every penny I possibly could so that we didn't go hungry while he attended Northeastern.

"I should have sent you to Suffolk," I growled at him. "At least then, I wouldn't have wasted a hundred grand so you could be a corrupt judge."

"I am not a corrupt judge!" Kenneth hollered. "What part of this don't you get?"

"All of it!" I shrieked. "How could you throw away fifteen years of marriage for a fling? Fifteen years, Kenneth! We were building a life together. We were supposed to have—"

"Have what, Shannon?" he demanded, stepping up into my personal space. Those deep brown eyes of his bore into my green ones with a fury I'd only seen him use on the worst criminals, the ones he absolutely loathed and could never be impartial to.

I guessed I fell into that category now. The category of "People Kenneth Loathes."

"Have… it!" I sputtered as I attempted to articulate just what "it" was. But I couldn't find the words. "It" was huge. "It" encompassed so much that I couldn't possibly do it justice with a few shouted sentences.

"Yeah," Kenneth sneered. "'It' being the fancy house, the nice car, the dog."

Kenneth pointed an accusatory finger at Marley, our mutt. We weren't exactly able to spring for the Golden Retriever six years before.

"What's wrong with that?" I demanded. "I wanted a nice life, a comfortable one. I wanted to be happy in my marriage, unlike every other woman in my family. Is that too much to ask?"

Kenneth stopped. A brief flash of humanity leapt into his eyes, but then it was gone just as quickly. I almost wasn't sure if it had actually been there in the first place.

"Maybe it is," he finally whispered, his eyes downcast. "Because by asking for it, you tried to mold me into something I'm not… Something I could never be for you."

"All I asked was for you to love me," I murmured. Tears pricked my eyes, and I felt the brick wall I'd so carefully built in the last two weeks start to crumble and fall.

"No, you didn't." He shook his head and adjusted his navy blue tie. "You asked me to be this monument of a husband—like I was some character in a storybook. This isn't a story, Shan."

"It's our story," I insisted. I stepped up to him and cupped his soft, warm cheeks in my hands the way I always used to, begging him to look up at me.

To love me.

But he didn't. Kenneth leaned into my touch one last time before he shoved my hands off of him and stepped back, teary eyed.

"It's your story," he replied. "I have to go live my own story. And you're just not in it. I'm sorry. Really."

And I could see that he was. He thought that his apology was enough to make me forget that after fifteen years, he'd come home one night and just asked me for a divorce. Just like that. No nonsense, no lead in.

Kenneth started to walk down the giant, carpeted staircase, making a beeline for the door. I did my best to force myself to stay put. I couldn't watch him leave this time.

But my feet had other plans. Before I knew it, I was out of our enormous master bedroom and pressed up against the railing of our second floor landing.

"Ken?" I called out, right as his hand went to open our massive oak front door.

He froze, hand in the air, and didn't turn back to me.

"What?"

"Why her?" I couldn't help it. I needed to know what was so much better about this other woman. What made her worthy of breaking up a marriage?

Kenneth sucked in a huge breath, and then sighed. He didn't turn to look back at me when he spoke. I wasn't sure if it was because he couldn't bear to see the look on my face, or if he didn't want me to see the look on his.

"She and I want to live the same story, Shannon."

With that, the door slammed shut with a sound of such finality, I swear it could have happened in a Hitchcock movie.

The scream that ripped from my throat was so feral and animalistic, it almost sounded like a banshee. Not that I believed in those sorts of things.

When all of the sound had made its way out of me, and my vocal chords had been just about rubbed dry, I slowly turned back to the bedroom, where I had about fifteen boxes full of clothes to seal and pack.

Except they were all done.

Every single box that I had packed up was closed and sealed nicely with two layers of tape, as if some invisible assistant had come along and finished the task for me in mere moments.

For a second, my heart stopped, and my heavy panting caught in my throat.

"You're imagining things, Shannon," I muttered to myself. "You must have closed those boxes already."

But how could I have? The last thing I remembered doing was yanking a Louboutin out of an open box to throw at Kenneth. Even the box of shoes, though, was closed and sealed.

Freaked out, I headed down to the kitchen to finish packing. The movers would be coming in the morning, and I'd be on a flight home the next afternoon.

Home.

I hadn't been there for more than a brief, two-day visit in nearly ten years. It wasn't that I didn't love my mom and my Grams, or Grams' best friend, Dina. I loved them more than words could say.

It was their beliefs I didn't love. All three of them were impossibly superstitious, and whenever I was around, I always felt like there was some big secret I was missing out on, some sort of major thing I just didn't know.

Which was crazy. They were my family, and I knew everything there was to know about them all.

But still. My intuition always went haywire whenever I was in that house, the same one Mom had grown up in after her father had abandoned them.

The same one I'd grown up in.

Less than twenty-four hours after my final fight with Kenneth, I was in an Uber and on my way to the airport.

And stuck in traffic.

"Are you sure there are no backroads you can take to get us there faster?" I asked the driver, a stout young man with fire engine red hair, the same color as mine. He had a South Boston accent, and drove with his golfing hat on backwards.

"No, lady, sorry," the guy shrugged. "Traffic's real bad out today, huh?"

"Sure is," I sighed, and looked at my watch for the fifth time in as many minutes.

I had half an hour before the gates closed, I missed my flight, and I was stuck in Boston for... who knew how long. I just needed to get out, to go home and see my family and make some sort of attempt to reconnect with life itself. Figure out my next act.

Without Kenneth.

The traffic didn't improve, even by a smidgeon. I was late to the airport, and by the time I made it through security, I was sweaty and anxious as I sprinted through the terminal.

Just as I got up to my gate, I saw those big white doors start to close.

"No, wait!" I screamed, so loudly I turned a plethora of heads. The attendant either didn't hear me or didn't care, because those doors closed all the same.

"I... have... a ticket... for this flight," I gasped at the cranky old flight attendant manning the door. "I need to get on."

She looked up, appraised me with dark hazel eyes, and then shook her head with absolutely no remorse.

"Sorry," she shrugged. "Can't help ya. Get here earlier next time, like everyone else."

"No, look, you don't understand," I wailed. I could already feel it all coming down on top of me, revving up for a massive breakdown. The cheating, the divorce, the move, the pre-mid-life crisis I was about to have. "I'm getting a divorce, okay? Because my cheating ex-husband has some grand idea that he's going to go live a story, whatever that means. But he's not just living a story. Oh, no. He is living it with *someone else.* The man cheated on me and then had the gall to blame it on this insane need to 'live my own story.' What does that even mean? Do you know? Because I don't. I just... don't. So anyways, now I'm here, trying to get on this flight to go home and see my Mom and my Grams—who I haven't seen since Christmas, mind you. I am a terrible daughter, I know, save it. My ex used to tell me that all the time. He also said I was a terrible spouse, but he's the one who cheated, so you tell me who got the last word there, okay? All I'm really saying is that I need, and I mean *need*, to get on this flight and get the hell out of this city before the whole thing falls down and suffocates me. So is that too much to ask, for you to open those doors and let me get on my flight so I don't suffocate?"

Yeah.

It wasn't until after I'd finished, and felt that sort of out of breath panic a person feels after they've acted like a total idiot, that I realized I'd pretty much just dumped my entire life story on a total stranger.

And an entire airport terminal.

The stewardess, though, looked wholly unimpressed and unamused with my story. She just shook her head and sighed.

"Go back to customer service and they'll get you on the next flight," she informed me. "Have a good day."

She glanced back down at whatever stupid paper was on her desk, and that was when I lost it.

"Listen to me!" I hissed, crouching down so I could meet her eyes head on. "You need to let me on that flight. Now."

All of a sudden, the woman's hazel eyes went blank, kind of like a person's does in an over-acted TV scene where they're supposed to be hypnotized. She stared at me, and this scary smile twitched the corner of her lips, but didn't go all the way, and sure as hell didn't meet her eyes.

"Okay, you can get on this flight," she said

11

robotically, and then went to open the doors as if she was a puppet on a string.

I didn't even have time to question the strange oddity. I just nodded my thanks and rushed past her to get on that plane.

2

THE FLIGHT WAS LONG. Mostly because I hated flying. Of course, one time I'd gone all the way from Boston to Australia, and made it out alive. I hadn't been too sure I'd step foot in Sydney, though, since the flight was so full of turbulence all I could do was replay the opening scene of *Lost* over and over and over in my mind.

I think it's safe to say I'm a bit of a wimp when it comes to planes. But, hey, a girl's allowed to have one fear, right? And since there was absolutely nothing else in the world that could possibly scare me, I allowed myself to panic whenever my plane hit a little pocket of air and shook like we were in the middle of freaking Pompeii.

I was still the first one to step off that flight, though. I pretty much rushed right to the front the moment we were allowed to unbuckle our seatbelts, carry on in hand. The flight attendants tried to tell me to sit back down but, once again, they seemed to listen to me. Who knew all it took to get your way was a bit of eye contact and some desperation fueled by an emotional breakdown?

My sudden powers of persuasion were notable, but I didn't have the energy or time to decipher why, because the plane had rolled up to the gate at that point, and I really wanted off.

And I needed to pee. Airplane bathrooms were not my favorite place in the world.

I dashed off the plane, went to the restroom, and then headed toward the parking lot, where my mom was supposed to meet me.

As long as she wasn't late. Which was, to be completely honest, an absolute rarity. Sometimes I wondered if I was secretly adopted, since I had this insatiable need to be everywhere at least five minutes early. Had it not been for the classic McCarthy red hair and green eyes, I would have already tried to search out some long lost birth parents.

See, the thing is, I'm nothing like Mom or Grams. In fact, I'm just about as opposite from them as a girl could possibly get. Whereas the women in my family tended to be a bit frazzled, always late, and sometimes forgot their heads were on their shoulders, I was a Type A, completely neurotic, perfectionist.

We butted heads a lot growing up. We butted heads even more when I went off to law school with grand ideas of helping people and making a lot of money. Grams and Mom see very little value in money. They would have preferred I'd stayed home, gone to the University of Oregon, and helped them run their tiny little occult shop on Fourth Street.

But I'd wanted no part in that. Magic doesn't exist, and I sure as hell didn't want to peddle falsities to the poor tourists. Mom and Grams didn't see it that way, of course. In their minds, crystals and herbs were full of mystical energy and all sorts of magical elements.

But our deviant beliefs weren't even the worst of it. No, that came when I met Kenneth. The thing is, Mom and Grams believed there was some sort of curse on our family. The men never stuck around, or they were absolutely worthless, or they died. And, admittedly, when I looked at our family history as it pertained to love and marriage, we didn't have the best track record.

Grams grew up with her mom, aunt, and cousin —all women, no men. Grams' dad had run out on them, while her uncle had been killed. Even her aunt's son had disappeared mysteriously. And when she'd come to Portland, something similar had happened to her.

I wasn't too clear on the details, though. The guy may have run out, or been killed, or, well, never existed for all I knew.

And then there was the story of my own father. A flighty hippie who would have rather smoked pot all day than raise a baby.

Now, the same thing had happened to Kenneth and me.

So, taking all of that into consideration, it almost did seem like we were cursed. But I'd never let them know I was starting to believe it, just a little bit. Especially after the blowout that happened when Kenneth and I had gotten married. They'd told me he wouldn't stick around, and I'd in turn said some equally unpleasant things.

But now, there I was, walking out into the bright sunshine of a summer's day in Portland, single and heartbroken, just as they'd said I would be.

I shook myself away from those thoughts and instead turned to search for my mom. It was no use anticipating what she might say before she'd even said it. No, it was better to just wait and see.

To my surprise, I spotted her in the twenty-minute pick up zone, leaning against the hood of her bright red, 1994 Mustang convertible, shades over her eyes and bright red lipstick on her full lips.

Classic Mom.

She looked up as I approached, and her red curls glinted in the sunlight. I noticed a few streaks of gray in them that I hadn't seen before, and realized with a start that my mom was getting older.

I was forty, after all. The woman was already sixty-five, though she didn't look a day over fifty. People tended to mistake us for sisters constantly.

"Hi, Mom," I greeted her as I mentally prepared myself for the avalanche of jabs at my broken marriage.

"Is that my baby girl?" My mom gasped playfully. She ripped her shades from her eyes and scrutinized me as if I was a piece of art in some big, famous museum. "Look at you, Ms. Shannon McCarthy!"

Jab number one. Regressing to my maiden name already.

"I see we've lost the 'Mrs.' title already," I joked.

"Baby, the man divorced you." She rolled her eyes and pulled a face at the thought of Kenneth. "Drop the M.R.S. Degree and get your ass back on the streets. Hell, if I still looked like you, that's where I'd be right now!"

"You look exactly like me," I laughed.

We were now face to face with each other, and my mom stopped to give me a real once over, the kind only a mother can give.

"How ya doing?" She asked softly, reaching out a hand to stroke my cheek.

The torrent of tears I'd been barely holding in for the last few weeks threatened to wash over me right then. There's something about a mother's touch that manages to bring out all of the suppressed emotions a girl would rather hide.

"Fine," I whispered, but we both knew it was a lie.

"Well, let's get home and see if we can improve upon 'fine,'" she announced, grabbing my carry on and tossing it carelessly into the back of her convertible. "Your Grams made chicken 'n' dumplings just for you."

"Grams cooked for me?" I asked in astonishment. I truly couldn't remember the last time the woman had made a meal that didn't come from a box. Grams could do it, no doubt, but she always said cooking felt like a waste of time when there was ready made food for sale in the supermarkets.

"Don't look so surprised when you walk in, kid," Mom instructed as she peeled away from the parking space and started to race down the street at top speed. That was how she always drove, and she'd never once gotten a ticket for it. My mom could talk her way out of any situation, even speeding tickets. "She's really proud of this meal, for whatever reason. Grams never cooked me food when I was heartbroken."

"Well, did you ever go through a divorce?" I shot back.

Elle McCarthy glanced at me out of the corner of her eyes like she wanted to say something, but then shut her mouth and turned back to look at the road.

That was weird. My mom never kept her mouth shut about *anything*. Hell, I knew every time she had a UTI.

And Grams had cooked.

I wasn't sure why, but a weird feeling settled in the pit of my stomach. Something was off, but I couldn't quite put my finger on it.

We pulled up to the quaint little cottage on the outskirts of Portland, and the jewel green door swung wide open to reveal Adora McCarthy in all of her glory. Her red hair had gone blonde and white with old age, and her porcelain skin sagged a bit at her neck and chin.

Her green eyes sparkled with the same youthful joy they had for as long as I could re-member. For a ninety-year-old woman, she acted like she was still in her sixties.

I had some darn good genes.

"My granddaughter is home!" Grams sang in her thick Southern drawl as I sprang from the car and dashed up to hug her. "It's a pity you had to come home because of that horrid man, but I'm still glad you're back."

"I missed you," I murmured into her hair. It smelled of lavender and patchouli oil, a scent combination that was uniquely Grams.

"Well, you should have come back to visit more often!" She exclaimed, swatting me softly on the shoulder.

"Mama, she couldn't, remember?" my mom replied as she marched through the door with my bag. "She was a big time D.A. in the city."

"Right, of course," Grams nodded seriously.

"It's much more important than helping us run our little shop."

There it was. Jab number two. There would be plenty more where that came from.

"Don't think about it like that," I chided her, stepping into the house myself. "Besides, all of that's in the past now."

I sucked in a deep breath, smelling the sage and herbs that I had grown up with. Crystals and occult trinkets littered the mantle in the living room, while charms to ward off Fae and other demons hung over every doorway. The place looked like an eclectic mess.

But it was the eclectic mess I'd grown up with. Even though I didn't believe in any of it, I still felt comforted by all of it, the way I had as a child. The charms and crystals and trinkets made me feel safe.

"Shannon, get your behind in this kitchen!" Grams called out. "The big city D.A. needs a home cooked meal."

"Coming!" I called out.

I had just turned to the kitchen when I heard a familiar meow behind me. I turned to see Gram's old cat, Herman, as he approached me, in the mood for our usual single pat greeting.

"Hey, buddy," I murmured as I bent down.

For the first time in my entire adult life, I suddenly realized just how strange it was that Herman was even... alive. That might sound absolutely horrible, but the cat had been around for as long as I had been around. Longer, even, since Grams had him before I was born.

I mean, the cat had to be at least forty. I'd never heard of a cat living that long in my entire life.

As if Herman could hear my inner musings, he reached up and swatted my knee with his sharp claws.

"Ouch," I hissed at him, instantly taking my hand back. "No pets for you if you're going to act like that."

"Meow!" Herman replied, before he stalked off with his tail held high.

"How the hell are you still alive?" I murmured when I watched him go.

I'd already seen too many strange things within the last day to give this seemingly immortal cat any more thought. So instead, I tried to shove the oddities out of my mind and turned back to the kitchen, where the aroma of freshly made chicken and dumplings filled my nostrils.

3

IT TOOK me less than a day to confirm that Mom and Grams were, in fact, acting extremely strangely. They made no more comments on my failed marriage. They didn't try to tell me that men were useless, or that marriage was a made-up institution meant to keep women down and allow the patriarchy to flourish, or even make a not-so-subtle hint that I'd picked a job that was far too demanding.

They were walking on eggshells because I was getting a divorce. Maybe they felt guilty that, after all of these years wishing Kenneth would step out of our lives, he finally was.

I was in my childhood bedroom, complete with drawings of fairies and a pink canopy bed, on my second morning in Portland when my mom knocked on the door.

As she had when I was a teenager, Mom knocked once and then proceeded to just open the door, without even waiting for me to tell her to come in.

"Please, do, enter," I said sarcastically.

"Privacy, sorry!" Mom put up her hands and then stepped back out into the hall dramatically. She closed the door and knocked again, but this time, she waited and didn't come in straight away.

I should have been used to her antics after dealing with them for forty years, but they still never ceased to make me laugh.

"You may come in," I called out, in my most posh voice.

"Why, thank you for allowing me entrance to your humble abode," Mom replied, in an equally posh voice, as she entered.

"You are quite welcome," I laughed. "What's up?"

"I was just wondering if you wanted to come down to the shop with us this morning," she replied. "It's a full moon, so we're expecting a bit of a rush. We could really use your help. I'll even pay you! You do need a job after all."

"Mom, I don't really think being a cashier is on my list of desirable jobs," I chuckled. I glanced down at the laptop in front of me, where I was searching for any and all law-related jobs in Portland and sighed. "I'd much rather be in the shop with you and Grams than going over this."

"What is it?" She asked curiously.

"Just a bunch of nothing," I replied. "I'm hoping some law firm needs a replacement, or one of the neighboring counties might need a criminal prosecutor."

"That stuff is just too awful," Mom sighed. "I don't know how you do it."

"Neither do I," I murmured, more to myself than anyone else. Sometimes, seeing criminals day in and day out really did get to me.

But of course, my mom's eyes immediately lit up as she latched onto my words.

"Do you think you might want to... quit? Find another line of work?" She asked hopefully.

I was about to say no, of course not, but something stopped me.

"Maybe," I sighed. "I just don't know what I'm doing anymore. At all."

We sat in silence for a moment. For the first time in her life, Elle McCarthy was speechless.

Not that I could blame her. I'd always had a plan for my life, up until now.

Now, I felt as if I was just floating through time and space, held down by nothing more than a loosely tied string that could fall away at any moment.

"Come to the shop," Mom ordered, patting my leg. "A little bit of magic makes everything better."

As was tradition, I rolled my eyes at that statement. But I couldn't help thinking that maybe I *was* in need of a little magic at the moment.

My mom hadn't lied.

The shop *was* busy. With the boom of millennial spiritualism and all those crazy people who believed in "woo" in the last ten or so years, business was better than ever. And, since Mom and Grams had a reputation among the Portland laypeople for being the go-to women on anything pagan, mystical, or magical, they had cornered the market long before those new, capitalist, fake shops could.

Not that I thought anything they sold was real. They just didn't fake it, since the two of them believed in it all so hard. They'd even named the shop "Magic for Real."

I spent the day reverting to my teenage self. But where I used to pack bags for cat ladies and strangely quiet people, I was now packing bags for young dudes in beanies and thirty-year-old moms with dyed blonde hair and vegan kale smoothies in hand. The crowd of customers had changed, but the shop sure hadn't. There were still hand-tied sage bundles near the register, potions along the shelves, and altars for sale in the back.

"Having fun?" Grams asked halfway through the day, when I'd just finished stuffing a bag full of crystals and spell candles for a twenty-something guy with fifty holes in his face.

"Of course," I replied with a smile, but it was a lie. I just wanted to placate my dear old grandmother.

She, of course, saw right through me.

"No, you're not," Grams chuckled. "I don't know why you never appreciated the magic in this store, Shannon, but after forty years, I certainly know you don't like it."

"It's not that I didn't appreciate it," I hedged. "I just... don't believe in it."

Grams paused and scrutinized me for a moment, in a way that made me feel like I was both under a microscope and naked in front of a crowd all at the same time, as if all of my secrets were stripped bare and displayed for everyone to see. It was... weird.

Her gaze trailed down to my hands, and for a moment, I could have sworn I saw her frown at them, as if there was something wrong.

Quickly, though, her green eyes snapped back to my face, and she managed a small smile.

"Of course you don't," she whispered.

Something in her tone told me she spoke more to herself than to me. Her green eyes glazed over for a moment, and she went somewhere far away. A split second later, she turned away from me and marched into the back.

"Close down the shop!" She called over her shoulder. "We're reducing our hours today. You can go home, Shannon. Lock the door on your way out, would you, please?"

Grams hadn't spoken to me like that since I was in high school. All of a sudden, I was reduced to a fifteen-year-old girl who was at the whim of her mom and grandmother again. Those old feelings came flooding back, and I realized exactly why.

Grams and Mom were hiding something from

me. They'd acted like this when I was in high
school, and they were doing it again. I'd never
been able to figure out just what it was they
hadn't told me when I was a teenager, but I sure
as hell wanted to try now. I was a full-grown
woman, for heaven's sakes! And a District Attorney! There was no reason they should hide anything from me.

I hurried to lock the door before any customers could come in, but instead of leaving, I
retraced Grams' steps and followed her into the
back of the warehouse, where the employee
break room was.

Not that anyone other than Grams, Mom, or
Dina ever used the place. The three of them had
never wanted to hire on any help, even when the
store became so popular it would have made fi-
nancial sense.

"No, we can't tell her that!" I heard my mom
hiss as I closed in on the break room.

Immediately, I stopped moving and opened
my ears, listening as hard as I could.

I really had reverted to a teenager.

"What do you mean, we can't, Elle?" That was
Dina. "How would you feel if we had never told
you?"

"Well, that would never have been an issue,

now, would it?" Mom demanded. "Because we all know what happened when I turned twenty-one. And, unless she's not telling us something, the same cannot be said—"

"What if that's the reason?" Grams asked. "You know what's been happening in this town. Don't you think it would be smart if there were more of us?"

"Of course I know what's been happening," Mom snapped. "I read the news."

My curiosity got the better of me in that moment. I wasn't proud of it, since I could tell this conversation was awfully private, but it seemed to involve me, somehow. And if I was involved, then I sure as hell deserved to know.

So, I stepped around the corner with my arms crossed over my chest.

"What's been happening in the news?" I asked.

Three wide sets of eyes met my own. Dina jumped up and pushed something behind her back, shielding it from my view, albeit not very well.

"Shannon!" Grams exclaimed. "I thought you went home already."

"Well, I was about to, until I heard you guys having some sort of secret meeting," I replied. "Spill. What's going on?"

They looked from each other, to me, and back again.

"Shannon, baby, why don't you go see your uncle down at the ice cream parlor?" Dina asked sweetly. "I'm sure he'd love to give you two scoops of your favorite ice cream!"

"Not cutting it, Auntie Deedee." I shook my head. "I deal with lying criminals day in and day out. I know when someone's hiding something. What's behind your back?"

On any other day, I would have felt awful for pushing them like this. It wasn't my place to try and get information from them when they so clearly didn't want to share.

But I was tired.

Tired of secrets, and lies, and late night meetings that I wasn't invited to. Tired of feeling like there was something missing in my life, like I didn't have a part of me readily available.

Like something was shut down inside of me.

They were all caught and, by the looks on their faces, they knew it, too. Slowly, as Mom vehemently shook her head and tried to make her stop, Deedee brought out the secret she'd shoved behind her.

It was a newspaper. She laid it flat out on the

faux wood break room table and stepped back, looking up at me nervously.

"Take a look at this headline."

I swear to God, I thought the damn thing was going to say that Kenneth had been murdered, or aliens had been discovered on Mars or, hell, that it turned out I was the Queen of Freaking England.

But the headline said none of those things. Instead, it blared: **Three Women Murdered, Police Have No Leads.**

"Oh, wow, that's, uh, really sad," I said, sort of in a state of shell shock. I was a D.A. I dealt with murder all the time, and often with the people who committed those crimes. As sad as it was, the three deaths of the Portland women didn't really affect me. "Did you know them?"

"Well, no," Mom hedged. Her green eyes went soft, though, like I would have expected if she actually did know them.

"Uh, okay, so why the big secret?" I was genuinely confused now. I'd lost all of the curiosity that had prompted me to come and investigate.

"Read further," Grams instructed with a nod toward the paper.

Still confused, but willing to listen, I glanced down and started to read the article.

There wasn't anything that would have suggested the need for such strange behavior. Three women had been murdered within the last week. They lived in different parts of town, worked at different jobs, and hung around in different social circles. The only thing that even tied these women together was the circumstances of their murders.

They'd each been tied up, and someone had carved a pentagram into their chest before driving a dagger through their hearts. The murder weapon had yet to be found.

"Geez," I breathed. "That's some serious psychosis. I'd bet the police are looking for a serial killer, white male, mid to late thirties."

I was met with only blank and confused stares.

"Typical serial killer M.O.," I shrugged. "Although the symbol thing is new. I've never dealt with a perp who did that before. It's probably some weird way for him to mark his territory and show off to the other serial killers."

"The... other serial killers?" If Mom's eyebrow had gone up any further, they would have disappeared right into her hairline.

"Yeah, there's a lot more of them out there than you might think," I told her seriously.

Again, the three of them shared what was probably meant to be a surreptitious glance, but came across as more of a worried, tense, three-way stare down that was very obviously not meant for my eyes. If I didn't know any better, I almost would have thought they were communicating telepathically.

"What is it?" I asked. "Do you know who did this, or something?"

"Of course not!" Deedee cried.

"So then what? Why are you all acting so strange?" I demanded.

Silence. Again. This time, I resolved to be silent, too, until somebody gave me some damn answers. I crossed my arms over my chest and planted my butt in one of the cheap folding chairs so I could glare at all three of them at the exact same time.

Finally, Grams let out a sigh and marched over to me, putting her hands on my cheeks so she could look me straight in the eyes.

"We're afraid we'll be next, pumpkin."

4

IF THERE HAD BEEN a mirror in front of me, I'm pretty sure the expression on my face would have been comical enough to make me burst out laughing. In one split second, I went through the wringer of emotions. I was dumfounded, shocked, surprised, tickled, and then, finally, absolutely certain that everyone around me had lost their damn marbles.

"You're afraid you'll be next?" I demanded, before the inner D.A. in me took hold and forced myself to calm down. I took a deep breath just like my yoga instructor taught us to, and then leveled Grams with an even stare. "What exactly would make you think that? Has someone threatened you? Were these women somehow associated with you?"

"They all shopped here," Mom offered.

Oh boy.

"Mom, you think that just because these women shopped in your store, an occult shop, something that has exploded in popularity over the last ten years, that the killer will target you next?" I asked diplomatically.

The logic wasn't there, in my mind. Their shop was so popular, I was almost certain everyone in Portland had shopped there at some point. The killer couldn't possibly be targeting every single woman in Portland. He probably had some other, twisted, insane criteria to judge who would be his next victim. All serial killers did.

"They were special," Auntie Deedee offered. "They came—"

"Deedee," Mom warned, her tone dark and dangerous. It was so scary, in fact, that it actually made my heart drop to my stomach. The last time she'd used that tone in front of me, she'd found out I'd lost my virginity to the high school bad boy, Frankie Sampson.

"They came what?" I asked quietly, nervously, hoping that somehow Deedee would be the only one able to hear me. Which was obviously impossible, seeing as we were all in the same room. But I was the kind of person who hated unclear endings. If someone started a sentence, I needed to know the end of it, no matter how bad it might be.

Like when you're at a party, and everyone's talking in one big group, and there's that one sort of quiet person who will start a sentence, and then not finish it because other people are talking over them, and poor Quiet Person decides what they have to say isn't worth anything. I was always the one who stopped the entire conversation just to hear what they had to say. It wasn't because I was trying to be particularly nice, although I did find it rude to just bulldoze people.

I was just too curious. It was a McCarthy curse.

Dina glanced from Mom, to me, and back again. She twisted her bottom lip in her teeth the way she always did when she was nervous before she finally shook her head.

"It's nothing," she hedged. "I'm just jumping to conclusions."

"All assumptions are valid until they've been disproven," I informed her, my D.A. hat jumping back onto my head again.

"Not in this house," Mom interrupted. "And

not in this store. You weren't supposed to hear this conversation, anyways."

"Why not?" I asked. "What's the big secret?"

"We just didn't want you to worry," Grams wrapped my hand in her own and looked into my eyes with such deep sincerity I almost believed her.

Almost.

"Are you sure?" I murmured.

"Of course." Grams nodded reassuringly. "These murders have just thrown us all off, just like they did last time. Things will go back to normal soon."

"Mama!" My mother gasped, but it was too late. The words were already out of Grams mouth, and I'd had plenty chance to process them.

"What happened last time?"

This was something none of them could talk their way out of. Grams' words were clear as day, and they knew it, too. Once again, they shared that same, surreptitious glance.

"What is it with the looks?" I demanded, throwing my hands up into the air. "Do you think I can't see it when you stare at each other like that?"

For emphasis, I made my eyes all big and googly-eyed to imitate the way theirs looked. Geez. Maybe I'd make a class all about how to lie like a criminal just so these three weren't so easily caught.

Although that probably wouldn't benefit me, since I was the one they'd be lying *to*.

"This happened before," Grams explained. Her green eyes glazed over, and she went far away as her memories washed over her. "The exact same events. We were all so terrified. The symbols in the chest... the ropes soaked in wolfsbane... the dagger to the heart... it was so terrible. I thought we'd never make it out alive. I was so afraid my child would be an orphan at the hands of some awful f—"

"Mama, remember who you're talking to," Mom suddenly warned.

Instantly, Grams snapped right back to the present. She pursed her lips and nodded seriously, all business once more.

"Of course, it might not be the same," she covered. "Now, Shannon, go run along and get some ice cream like your Auntie Deedee told you to. We've got to do inventory."

"Well, I can help—"

"No, no you can't." Mom put her hands on my shoulders and started to shove me out of the

39

break room roughly. "Inventory is too precious a thing. Go have some ice cream. We're going to pick up Gino's for dinner, and we'll be back at the house around six."

And with that, the break room door slammed in my face. I was, quite literally, nose to nose with its peeling green paint as I stood there in slight shock for about three seconds.

Then, I got really suspicious. Now, I loved my mom, Grams, and Auntie Deedee. They had a lot of admirable qualities, too. But seriousness was absolutely not one of them. And speaking to me like actual parents should was also not my mom's strong suit.

So the combination of those two extremely unusual traits suddenly making an appearance had me on high alert.

Suffice it to say, I did not go down to the ice cream parlor and have a big, fat scoop of the icy deliciousness. I wasn't a teenager anymore, and I certainly didn't live under their roof. What was the worst they could do to me? I was a grown woman, and I had the right to make my own decisions.

Decision number one: time for snooping.

Any records of these first murders were almost definitely not on my dear friend Mr.

Google's website. If it was before I was born, and back when my mother was still young enough to have been an orphan if things went sideways, then that meant I was looking for articles from the late 1940s to the early 1960s.

So, as I had many times as a bored teen, I walked down to the Portland library and headed into their Records section. Although this time, I wasn't looking for articles to write my next history paper.

"Hello," the sultry, elderly librarian greeted me from behind her massive Coke bottle glasses. Even that heavy of a prescription wasn't enough for her, though, because her hazel eyes were focused on a spot just over my left shoulder.

"Hi," I gave her a little wave to try and help out her eyesight a little bit, but it did nothing. "I was wondering if you have any records of newspaper articles between, uh, 1947 to 1963 or so?"

"We do," she nodded.

And then didn't move.

"Can I see them?" I asked slowly.

"Sure," she shrugged.

But still didn't move.

"Okay, where are they?" I prompted, thinking I'd somehow ended up in the wrong section.

"I've got them in this computer here." She

pointed at her dinosaur era desktop. "But you'll have to be more specific. What exactly are you looking for?"

I thought about it for a moment.

"Anything on occult murders," I finally said. "Women who had symbols carved into their chests before they were killed."

The librarians eyebrows knitted together in distress.

"I remember that," she murmured quietly. "And now it's happening again to us."

"Who's 'us'?" I just about jumped on her language.

A flash of worry leapt into the old woman's eyes, but she shook her head quickly.

"The people of Portland, dear," she said sweetly. "What happens to one of us happens to all of us."

I had a feeling that was not at all what she had meant, but I didn't press the issue. I was tired of asking for answers and receiving nothing in return.

The librarian printed out the three articles that had been written about the murders and handed them to me with a perky smile I had a feeling she normally didn't wear.

But I smiled and thanked her, taking my

copies of the articles quickly, and retreating to my absolute favorite coffee shop.

Truthfully, I had no idea what I was doing. I wasn't the Portland D.A--and even if I was, it wasn't exactly in my job description to investigate things like this. But something inside of me-- call it intuition, call it curiosity, call it morbid fascination--knew that I needed to figure this out.

I was being lied to. Or, at the very least, information was being withheld. And, since it appeared I was the only sane person left on the entire planet, it was up to me to figure it out.

5

ROCKSTAR COFFEE HAD LONG BEEN a staple for Portland natives. I'd spent many a rainy day afternoon there while I was in high school, studying my math textbook.

And Jerry Abrams.

He'd been the cute, college-aged barista all of the girls were absolutely obsessed with. Of course, Jerry was a lot more interested in the bored stay at home moms than he was the silly high school girls, but we deluded ourselves into completely ignoring that fact.

When I walked into Rockstar Coffee, though, I got quite the shock. Gone were the kitschy metal tables and very simple coffee bar that pretty much just served drip coffee with milk and baked goods. The checkered, black and white tile floor had been ripped up and replaced, and the jukebox that had made it such a popular hangout spot in the mid-nineties had also been dumped somewhere else.

Now, Rockstar Coffee, albeit still under the same name, looked just like every other hipster coffee shop in Portland. It was filled with those awful, sustainable wooden tables surrounded by benches instead of chairs, meant to encourage people to share seats and talk with strangers. The coffee bar was now a full-blown espresso bar, complete with a shiny, stainless steel machine and three haphazard baristas with faces full of metal jewelry.

"Welcome to Rockstar Coffee," the pimple faced cashier greeted me with the same level of bored indifference all teenagers seemed to show nowadays. "What can I get you?"

"Uhh..." I took a moment to look at the menu, which was now two whiteboards filled with an assortment of different drinks with strange names, like "zebra mocha" and "caramel frappe."

"All of our drinks can come hot or blended," he prompted me, clearly wanting to move on to helping the customers in the line that had formed behind me.

"Right." I nodded. "Can I just get a dark roast drip coffee? With cream?"

I swear to God, the kid stared at me like I'd just jumped straight up from hell right in front of him.

"You just want a drip coffee?" He repeated in astonishment.

"Yeah. Do you guys not have that here?" It was a genuine question, since he was currently staring at me like I'd grown six heads.

"No, we do," he replied, before turning to holler over his shoulder in a voice that was the exact opposite of inside, "Dark drip!"

"Coming up!" The barista hollered back, her voice even louder than his.

"That'll be four twenty-seven," he told me.

"Four twenty-seven? For a cup of coffee?" I gasped.

Back home, I could get the same thing for a buck.

"Yeah," he nodded.

I shelled out the cash, retrieved my lukewarm cup of coffee, and sat at the only table meant for one person in the entire place. It seemed to be the one people had avoided so they could opt for "social inclusion," but I wanted to include absolutely nobody in my small social circle here.

I spent the next hour poring over the three articles in front of me. By the second, that strange feeling in my gut grew stronger and stronger, but I had no idea what the hell it was trying to point me to.

The previous murders had happened in 1955. There had been twelve altogether, which was a pretty damn big number considering they were all in the same city within a relatively short time frame. Six months, to be exact.

Just as Grams had mentioned, the murders were the exact same as the ones happening now. Each woman had been bound in her bed, carved up like a piece of meat, and then stabbed through the heart one singular time.

It seemed, though, that the reporters in 1955 were a lot more open to interviewing the crazy people than reporters today were. I knew this because, in the second article detailing the murder of Geneva Montcliff, a relatively wealthy high society woman, the reporter more or less alluded to the fact that Geneva was a witch.

Actually, taking into account the fact that she included a quote in which a "close acquaintance" of Geneva said: "She was a witch. She was always doing spells and making potions. The woman was killed due to prejudice against her kind, plain and simple," I was pretty sure the reporter was *definitely* saying that Geneva Montcliff was a witch.

To me, it seemed like Ms. Henrietta Jenkins, reporter for the *Portland Gazette* back in 1955, was very sure Geneva was killed for her supposed witchy powers.

Something struck me as I re-read that article about ten times. The way the librarian had said "us," and the way Grams had been so sure they were next... since it had happened before...

"No way," I breathed. "No way! This is crazy."

Thankfully, not a single person in the coffee shop looked up at my sudden outburst. Not that I would have cared. Inner turmoil had taken over and washed me in the choppy waters of absolute doubt.

This was all too much. My mind was putting things together that just weren't there. Witches didn't exist--real ones, anyway. If Geneva had gone around calling herself a witch, it was probably just because she was into those moon rituals and love spells, or whatever.

For all of that logic to add up, I had to ignore the tiny voice in my head that pointed out how, back in 1955, moon rituals and love spells weren't exactly the pop culture craze they were today. In fact, when Grams had opened her occult shop a few years later, she'd been looked at like a crazy woman until the hippies started to take over in the sixties.

Shaking my head, I flipped to the third and final article. I didn't even know why I kept reading at that point. None of this concerned me, really. Why was I so obsessed with a string of murders that had happened nearly fifty years ago? Either the killer was back again, probably in the form of some decrepit old man attempting to re-live his glory days, or we had a copycat. These news articles alone provided enough information for any run-of-the-mill crazy person to reenact the murders.

Right?

I was trying to convince myself at that point.

Suddenly, out of the corner of my eye, I caught a stranger passing by my table, awfully close by the standards of the modern day. He glanced down rudely at the papers splayed across my table as he walked by, and I heard a sound catch in his throat.

Great, he probably thought I was insane, too.

Then, he stopped about a foot past me, back-tracked slowly, and proceeded to stand right next to me staring down at the documents in front of me. I tried to give him a sort of sideways glance as I took a sip of my now cold coffee, but my usual side eye didn't do its job, and the guy just kept right on staring at me.

Finally, when I had just worked up enough annoyance to tell him to go away and get his nose out of my business, he spoke.

"You think there's a connection too, don't you?"

His voice stopped me in my tracks. Or I assume it would have, if I'd been walking. I wouldn't say it sounded like honey, or any of those cliched things women always say when they meet a new guy. In fact, he didn't even possess a particularly nice voice to listen to.

But there was something about the deep gravity, the way he formed every single word with careful precision, the way the sound seemed to roll over my eardrums like a welcome massage at the end of a very long day, that managed to hook me so insanely fast I didn't even know what he said to me.

"What?" I demanded, snapping my neck up to look fully at him.

The man didn't even flinch when I moved abruptly, though, which was all the more beneficial for me, because I got a perfect view of his roughened features.

He didn't look like the kind of man to frequent a Portland hipster coffee shop. He didn't even look like the kind of man who would be *in* Portland. He had a long, manly nose, and what I assumed was a perfectly chiseled jaw hidden under his bushy brown beard. Come to think of it, he looked a lot like the cowboys I'd see in old TV shows.

An all-American man.

The man in question flashed his light grey eyes at me and shot me a half smile.

"You always talk to strangers this way?" he asked.

"What way?" I snapped, before I caught myself. "Oh... uh, no, sorry. I just wasn't expecting anyone to ask me about these." I gesticulated wildly toward the papers spread out in front of me.

"When I see a normal citizen taking an interest in my case, I've got to ask," he shrugged.

"Your case?" My eyebrows nearly shot into my hairline. "Are you a detective?"

"Something like that."

There was something in his response that didn't quite sit well with me. The way his eyes left mine when he answered forced me to wonder what this man was, and, more importantly, *who* he was.

Until, of course, I reminded myself that it didn't at all matter to me. I was just doing some reading, nothing more. It wouldn't matter if this guy was the killer himself, so long as he didn't target me.

"May I sit down?" He asked.

Before I could answer, he went right ahead and sat down in the seat across from me.

"I didn't say yes," I said quickly.

"But you would have," he replied with a shrug and a knowing grin.

Even though he was right, this little attitude of his ticked me off.

"Look, I'm just doing some reading out of curiosity," I told him. "I've got no interest in this case."

"Seems to me like you do," he declared. "If you didn't, you wouldn't have gone to the trouble of going down to the library and looking up articles from forty-five years ago."

Instinctively, I shoved the papers away from me as if to show that I didn't care about what they said. To my absolute shock, as I did, this completely random stranger reached out and grabbed my hand in his own.

For a split second, I was paralyzed. His hand was warm and rough, and fit over mine in a way that reminded me so much of Kenneth I felt my heart crack just a little bit. Even more, though, I was entranced by those steely gray eyes in front of me as they bore into my own, almost as if he was looking right into the deepest, most well hidden parts of my soul.

Like a plane crash, I came back down to Earth and yanked my hand from his.

"What are you doing?" I demanded.

My tone was meant to send this stranger into a fit of embarrassment, but instead, he looked... interested? I wasn't even sure how to describe the expression on his face.

"Just introducing myself," he replied. "I'm Hunter. And that's my case you're looking at."

I glanced down at the papers in front of me, taking in the perfect, inky black typeface and the black and white picture of the scene outside of Geneva's mansion, and then back at Hunter.

"You're a cold case cop?" I asked.

"Not exactly," he replied. "I've been hired by a private firm to look into the recent murders here in Portland. You're not the only one to tie these two events together."

"Well, actually..." I was about to tell him that it was Grams who'd made the connection, not me, before I thought better about it. My heart might have started to lust after Hunter and his steely gray eyes, but my mind still knew enough to remind me not to tell a perfect stranger my business.

Even if that business was an insane curiosity with murders that happened nearly fifty years prior.

"Actually what?" He prompted.

"Actually, I have to go," I said abruptly, gathering up my papers into a haphazard pile and heading straight for the door. "I've got someone I have to meet."

"I thought you might want to talk about the case, though." Hunter stood up in a flash and blocked my path in a way that should have sent me into a fit of indignation. And it probably would have, if I hadn't noticed the way he smelled like a perfectly smoky campfire.

"I'm not a P.I." I shook my head. "Good luck figuring it out."

And with that, I ran out of the coffee shop and

onto the street. Something about Hunter gave me the heebie jeebies.

But something else about him made me want to sit down and talk to him for hours on end. Somehow, that was even worse.

6

I DON'T KNOW HOW, but my encounter with Hunter had shaken me up.

Nothing ever shook me up.

There was just something about him, but I couldn't put my finger on it. It wasn't necessarily bad, I didn't think. It was more like… intriguing. I wanted to know more about him. That, I could not have. No way was I about to let myself get entangled, in any way, with another man after what Kenneth had done.

Even if that man could answer some semi-burning questions I had about this case. The D.A. in me knew that Hunter probably had a lot of information tucked away in his brain. P.I.s always did. Most of the time, they even knew more than the cops did.

I had to get Hunter, and this case that wasn't even mine to begin with, off of my mind. I was walking down the street, hell bent on getting as far away from the coffee shop as I possibly could, when a tiny little bookstore caught my eye. It was new, I could tell, since the sign was still bright and shiny, which was a near impossibility after more than a season of Portland rain.

Stuffing the papers deep into my bag, I ducked into the shop. Why I didn't just toss them in the trash, I had no idea. This case was stuck with me, but that didn't mean I had to like it.

A tiny, brass bell clanged over the door as I entered, and I was immediately hit by the musky, aged aroma of old books and yellowed paper.

God, I loved that smell. It reminded me of childhood, and rainy days spent alone in the library with nothing but a stack of good books to keep me company.

"Hello, can I help you?" The salesclerk, a woman who looked to be about my age, approached me with a smile. She had dirty blonde hair that had been twisted into dreadlocks, a huge hoop through her septum, and wore a bright purple, floor length dress that looked as if it belonged in the seventies.

"I'm just browsing," I told her politely.

"Of course," she nodded. "Is there any particular genre—"

Suddenly, the woman's smile fell flat, and her feet faltered. She froze about six feet away from me, and her light brown eyes went wider than cantaloupes.

"Oh my," she breathed.

Instantly, I whipped around, terrified she'd seen something behind me.

But the store was empty, save for a group of middle school kids messing around in the science fiction section to my right.

"Is something wrong?" I demanded worriedly.

"I just... your energy is so..." her words trailed off, and she just continued to stare at me in a way that bordered on rude.

"My energy is what?" I prompted.

Before she could say another word, there was a loud crash, and a gasp from the boys.

"Dude, what the heck?" One of the kids cried. The saleswoman's gaze snapped away from me to take in the kids, who had managed to knock over two entire stacks of precariously displayed books.

"Boys, what did I say earlier?" She demanded as she swept over to go and fix their mess.

Leaving me totally in the dark as to what was so off about my 'energy.'

Shrugging, I continued on through the shop, chalking it up to yet another Portland hippie acting just a little bit strange.

The layout of the shop made absolutely no sense, so I decided to just start at the back and work my way forward, browsing for something interesting to occupy my mind while I tried to figure out my next move.

In the very back of the shop, right next to the section of strange looking cookbooks with yellowed pages that signaled their age, was a section that had been walled off with a bright, clean white curtain. It was a strange thing to see in a bookstore. Curiously, I pulled the curtain aside with one hand, wondering what needed to be shielded from the eyes of the customers.

And what I saw behind the curtain looked way too much like Mom and Grams' shop for my comfort.

So of course, I stepped inside. Reining in my curiosity had never been my strong suit.

The occult section, though out of place in this small bookshop, was organized and filled with objects I recognized which meant, as far as fake magic went, the person who owned this place knew what they were doing. There were crystals and potions, runes and necklaces for protection, and a plethora of other objects that, to the untrained eye, would have seemed just weird. But, growing up with the owners of an occult shop had taught me what each item was for.

There was a barrel of wolfsbane with a scoop in it, so curious customers could bag their own. And just past that was a little shelf, with a row of pictures and three lit candles. It looked sort of like a shrine.

As I got closer, I realized that it actually was a shrine, dedicated to the three women who had been murdered recently. There was a picture of each one of them behind a lit candle and surrounded by a circle of pure white salt.

"Strange," I murmured aloud.

I'd never seen anything quite like it, even at home, with Mom and Grams doing all sorts of strange things and calling them "rituals" or "spells." I couldn't tell exactly what the benefit of it was for. I knew that candles were meant to signal light and protection, and salt was also for protection.

Maybe these women had all been regulars at

the store? Either that, or whoever had created this little altar just wanted to pray for them. It was nice, I supposed.

But what wasn't nice was the table on the other side of the shelf. It was one of those entryway tables, with a purple cloth laid over it. On top of the table were ten more pictures, but these ones didn't have frames. Instead, they were laid out next to each other, forming a pentagram, and surrounded by a circle of candles. In between each photo was a little rock with a Celtic rune carved into it.

My feet carried me forward so I could get a better look at the ten photos on display. As soon as I did, my heart froze in my chest, and a shiver of strange fear undulated through my body.

I recognized two of the pictures. One was a photo of my Grams from about ten years before. She was smiling in it, but I could tell the picture had been blown up, like someone had gotten it off of Facebook. The second one was of my mom. It was a picture I'd taken, at my wedding.

There was a third picture there, too, of the woman who had greeted me.

I wasn't at all sure what I was seeing, but something in me wanted to reach out and touch the photos, to feel the smoothness of the paper under-neath my fingertips, almost like I wanted to make sure the women were safe within the confinements of the photographs. I watched my hand reaching out toward the little altar, but the moment I crossed the ring of candles, my entire arm was shocked, as if a bolt of lightning had struck down and run up my appendage, and then my body was shoved backward by an impossibly strong force.

The flames of the candles leapt five feet into the air with a flickering roar, lighting the room in a dance of orange and red that terrified me to the core. I gasped in shock as I stumbled backward, at once terrified and disbelieving.

"Ow!" A woman's voice cried as I stepped on her foot in my haste to escape the giant flames.

"Sorry!" It was a reflex apology. I spun around to find the saleswoman behind me, staring me down with that same confused and intrigued ex-pression.

"What did you do?" She gulped, staring at the flames.

"You see them, too?" I needed to convince my-self I wasn't a total lunatic.

As she nodded, the flames shrunk back to a normal size, the room went back to the drab white color, and the lightning evaporated from my arm.

"What have you done?" She demanded again. Suddenly, the sweet, if strange demeanor she'd held before disappeared, replaced with a thunderous anger.

"Nothing!" I cried out as she rushed past me and hunched over the table, searching to fix whatever I had screwed up.

I took the opportunity to get the hell out of Dodge. I had no idea what had just happened, and I didn't plan on sticking around long enough to find out. There wasn't any way I could have convinced myself that my eyes were playing tricks on me.

I knew what I saw. One second, those flames were a half inch tall, and the next, they were high enough to scorch the ceiling. For the umpteenth time, the strange, nervous feeling returned to my gut, and I was faced with the immense, unbearable notion that there was something I was missing, something I wasn't being told.

And whatever it was, those murders were connected to it somehow. Three dead women, and ten other women in those photos. If I hadn't seen a picture of the saleswoman herself, I might have wondered if she was the killer, and those were her targets.

But she wouldn't be targeting herself.

I came home to a quiet house. Mom and Grams were both in the kitchen, but neither one of them made a sound as I blew past them and into my bedroom. I couldn't focus on a conversation with them just yet. There were too many thoughts and questions swirling around in my own brain.

The first of which was the insatiable need to investigate this case. Somehow, Mom and Grams were connected to it. They were afraid they'd be next, and I had to make sure that didn't happen.

I didn't have to believe in magic and witches to know that there was a killer on the lam, targeting women in Portland. And somehow, the dead women were connected to my family.

Stressed, I tossed my bag into the corner of my room, and then threw myself down on the bed so I could stare up at the ceiling in a moment of sultry, teenage-like angst. I rolled over and stared at the papers spilling out of the khaki brown bag, pure and white, and full of a mystery from decades ago. There was not a doubt in my mind that everything was connected. I just wasn't sure why yet.

As I lay there, pondering, I noticed a tiny, creamy piece of paper that stood out from the others.

Curiously, I got up to go and see what it was. Picking it up, I could tell it was a business card with a name on it.

Hunter Black.

Right underneath that was a phone number. Somehow, the sneaky bastard had managed to slip this card into my things without me even realizing it. Which, I supposed, was a good thing. A P.I. seemed like just the kind of friend I needed.

Quickly, I yanked out my cell and dialed the number. That familiar, gruff voice picked up the phone.

"Hunter Black, private investigator."

"Sneaky little trick, sticking your card into my stack of papers," I told him.

"Ahh, mystery girl, I was wondering when you'd call," he chuckled. "Finally decided you wanna talk to me about this case?"

"Not exactly," I shot back. "I want to propose a mutually beneficial relationship. We work together to figure this thing out."

"Why are you suddenly so involved?"

"Let's just say, this case got personal, and leave it at that," I replied. "You in or you out?"

"I don't work in teams," he replied. "Especially with people I don't know."

"Look, I'm a D.A., okay?" I hadn't wanted to pull out my resume like that, but I couldn't think of another way to get this guy to let me team up with him. I didn't blame him for being hesitant, but that also wasn't my biggest concern. Right now, I just needed to get his knowledge and expertise.

"Yeahhh, D.A.s don't work with P.I.s." I could almost hear him shaking his head.

"Listen, I'm going to keep calling you until you say yes," I sighed. "So either you give in now, or get ready to have your phone bombarded."

There was a long pause on the other end of the line. I was nervous I'd pushed him too far, that he'd say no out of spite and just leave it at that.

But then, finally, he let out a single, low whistle.

"Alright, Ms. District Attorney," he said. "You've got yourself a deal. Meet me tomorrow. Rockstar Coffee. One p.m."

And then he hung up the phone.

A proud grin spread over my lips, and I caught a glimpse of myself in the mirror that hung next to the bed.

I looked alive. Really, truly alive. There was a sparkle in my green eyes that hadn't been there in a long time, and a flush to my usually pale cheeks.

I'd moved back to Portland to find the woman I'd lost. It looked like she was starting to come back to me.

7

I PULLED up to Rockstar Coffee in my Mom's Mustang precisely five minutes before one p.m. the next day. Mom, of course had been very nosy, and attempted to ask me all sorts of questions about where I was going and what I was doing, as if I was still in high school.

I managed to artfully avoid all of her queries and ducked out while she and Grams were in the middle of a rather heated discussion about whether or not they should change their crystal supplier. Apparently, there was a woman who trekked up and down the Western part of Africa once a year, gathering crystals from different places, and Grams wanted to buy her entire stock out. Mom, on the other hand, thought the woman's crystals were far too expensive.

As far as I was concerned, they were just a bunch of really pretty rocks. It shouldn't matter if they came from Africa or Lake Tahoe.

Or did it? Admittedly, after the last two days, I was a little unsure. The tick of my blinker blurred into the background as I thought over everything that had happened this week.

The boxes that had closed by themselves. The way people had seemed to listen to me on my flight. The weird conversation Mom, Dina, and Grams had in the break room the other day.

I was convinced I still didn't know the whole story on that one.

And then, lastly, there was the experience I'd had in the tiny back room of the bookshop yesterday. The one with the giant candle flames and the lightning in my arm.

I was so distracted with my tumultuous thoughts that I didn't even realize the little Honda Civic, whose spot I had been so patiently waiting for, had pulled away from the parking space, and I was now just blocking the street. As I pushed the gas down to park, a pristinely cleaned white Tesla whipped out from behind me, tires squealing, and shot into the spot faster than I could blink.

Out stepped an overly thin woman in a couture skirt and blouse that was probably worth more than the car I was driving.

"Hey! That was my spot!" I yelled at her.

But the woman didn't even bother to give me so much as a shrug. She just stepped up on the curb in her five-inch tall stilettos and marched into the real estate office next to the coffee shop.

"I hate people," I murmured under my breath. "I hope she pops a tire today."

POP!

The loud noise was followed by a gush of air. I watched in shock as the back left tire on her fancy car slowly sank down until it was completely flat.

I think my jaw hit the floor. I was so amazed I couldn't even feel my body anymore.

"It was just a coincidence." Trying to convince myself was no use, and I knew it.

But I did it anyway.

I drove on in a haze of quiet shock and found a parking space halfway down the block. At that point, I was late, but I couldn't even find it in myself to care when I walked in, and Hunter tapped his shiny silver watch mockingly.

"You're late," he said as I sat down. He shoved a coffee mug toward me, black, with no cream and sugar, and then leaned back in his chair to give me a once over.

"Someone stole my spot," I told him, absently taking a sip of my coffee.

Which was ice cold.

"Excuses, excuses," he sighed.

"Well, the least you could have done is give me a warm drink," I choked, setting the cold beverage down. Cold coffee had never been my thing.

"Are you sure it's cold?"

"Huh?" I asked. Hunter raised a brow and nodded at my coffee mug. Glancing down, I found that the beverage was now steaming, as if it had come out of the pot two seconds before.

Okay. Either I was losing it, or something else was going on.

Honestly, I wasn't sure which option I liked more.

"Let's just get to this case," I said. "What did you want to ask me yesterday?"

"Who says I wanted to ask you anything?" He shrugged casually.

"You did." I replied bluntly. "Yesterday."

"No, I just wanted to hear your thoughts," he grinned, a lopsided sort of smile that made my stomach twist up in a good way. "So go ahead. Share with the class."

I gave him a once over. Now was the time to really make my decision. Did I want to talk to this complete stranger about a case that I had some sort of connection to, one that I wasn't even sure of myself?

Yes. I did. Because I wanted to know all the details, and no cop would ever give those to me.

We spent the next two hours talking about the case, and the potential connections I'd made. Hunter explained that the person who'd committed the murders back in 1955 had never been found, and that the case remained open to this day.

Mostly, though, he observed me. He was good about it, subtle, attempting to watch me in a way that would have been invisible to most other women. But I'd spent years working with criminals, learning to observe their behavior, and learning how they observed mine.

Hunter wanted something. That was the only thing I was sure of when I walked out of that cafe. Just what that was, I had no idea.

I couldn't sleep that night. So, as any sane woman would, I pulled out pictures of the dead women and started to examine them, looking for anything Hunter or the cops might have missed, anything out of the ordinary.

Anything that would tell me why there had been a shrine to those women in the bookstore. Or why my grandmother was convinced that she'd be the next woman killed.

But I couldn't find a damn thing. I looked, again, at the picture of the first of these recent killings.

The woman was named Muriel Clarke. She was thirty-five, single, and a social worker. Muriel had dedicated her life to saving children from abusive situations, and finding them good, safe homes to live in.

Why someone would want to kill a saint like her was absolutely beyond me.

I leaned over the picture again, staring at her dead body, splayed on the bed, with that awful symbol carved into her chest. I hadn't even bothered to question Hunter when he'd revealed these photos to me. They were evidence in what I had started to consider "my case," and I'd take whatever I could get.

"Who did this to you?" I murmured to Muriel's dead body. Carefully, I stroked a finger down the smooth photo paper as a wave of sadness threatened to overtake me.

Abruptly, the space around me shifted, and within a second, it was as if I wasn't in my own room anymore.

I was standing in Muriel's bedroom. I recognized it from the photograph. There was the photo of Marilyn Monroe that hung over her bed, the pink curtains over her windows and…

"Oh my God!" I screeched.

Muriel was on the bed, underneath a dark, hooded figure as it tied her wrists to the bedposts. She was screaming and crying, begging her killer to spare her life.

"Stop!" I bellowed. "Get off of her!"

But it was as if I wasn't even there. Neither one of them seemed to hear me. Desperately, I tried to move, to run over there and help her, but I couldn't. My feet were glued to the faux hardwood floors of her apartment.

The killer said something then, in another language. I couldn't quite make out the words, but it sounded like Spanish, maybe? Or Latin of some sort?

Muriel kept struggling, but the killer grabbed her mouth and shoved in a tiny, tulle bag filled with what looked to be a mixture of herbs.

"What is that?" I murmured, trying and failing to step closer.

And then, just as quickly as it had come, the vision was gone, and I was back in my own room once more.

I gasped as my familiar walls fell back into place. I could feel the cool softness of my comforter underneath me, could smell the soft lavender of the calming spray Grams misted over our pillows every day, and yet, I still felt as if I was in that room with Muriel, listening as she begged a psychotic stranger to spare her life.

And as he denied her.

Those screams would haunt me forever. Tears streamed down my cheeks, but I didn't make a sound.

What the hell had I just seen? I didn't even know if it was real, or the product of some over exhausted nightmare brought on by stress and overwork.

I grabbed my phone, which was perched on the antique bedside table, and shot off a quick text to Hunter, praying relentlessly that he told me I was foolish.

Were any of the victims found with a bag of herbs in their mouths?

Those three little bubbles appeared to indicate

he was typing, and I held my breath as I awaited his response. I wasn't even sure what I wanted him to say.

Then, his response came in.

Yeah. How did you know?

I don't know how long I stared at those five little words. It might have been two seconds or two hours. But I couldn't even bring myself to respond.

"This is crazy," I chided myself. "Crazy! There is no way..."

The word wouldn't even leave my lips.

Magic.

I was starting to believe that magic was real. That the little potions and sage bundles Mom and Grams sold were a smidge more than funny trinkets.

I needed tea. I wasn't a huge tea drinker, normally, unless I was super stressed. When I was a child, Mom had always made me a cup of her "special tea," and it would calm me down within seconds. That was what I needed, because I felt the exact opposite of calm. In fact, I felt like I was going to rip out of my skin if I thought about the absolute insanity that had invaded my mind any longer.

I padded down the stairs and headed for the kitchen, assuming everyone else was asleep. Herman meowed softly from his cat tree by the window, but he didn't bother to get up.

Even the cat knew it was late.

Apparently, though, my mother did not. I caught a flash of her curly red hair as I rounded the doorway, but she didn't even see me.

Her back was to me, and she was standing at the old, temperamental stove that sometimes liked to just stop working for absolutely no reason at all.

"I hate you, you silly old thing," she snapped. "I always have to do everything myself."

As if to prove her point, she raised her hand in the air, snapped her fingers, and then threw a tiny ball of fire at one of the gas burners, lighting it up.

I'm pretty sure that's when I fainted.

8

I'D NEVER FAINTED before in my entire life.

Fainting's not nearly as normal as TV and movies make it seem, seeing as I'd gone forty years without doing it. But, apparently, seeing my mother snap her fingers and create fire out of thin air was just the kick in the ass I needed to turn into some swooning 1950s housewife.

Admittedly, the colors that were dancing behind my eyelids, as I was vaguely aware that I had slipped out of consciousness, were a lot more appealing than what I would see when I came back to the world of the waking.

Until, of course, someone shoved a vial of smelling salts under my nose, and I was rudely brought back to the real world by the abhorrently strong scent of eucalyptus and peppermint.

When I opened my eyes, the very first thing I noticed was the intense, bright lights above me. They came into focus slowly, and I could see that I was lying on the kitchen floor, under the fluorescent recessed lights Mom had installed three years ago.

The next thing I saw were the two very worried faces of Mom and Grams, hovering over me like they were afraid I was about to up and die on them.

"Oh my God!" I bellowed when the memories of the last few minutes came flooding back into my head. I shoved myself away from them, sliding backwards on my butt across the kitchen floor until my back slammed into the hard wood of the kitchen doorway.

"Shannon, calm down," Mom said, her voice uncharacteristically calm. "You just fainted."

"Yes, I did." I nodded vigorously, making some sort of attempt to process what I had just seen, while also trying to look like I hadn't already been wondering if magic was real.

Admittedly, I kind of wanted the high ground of feeling like I'd been lied to for forty years, and had held no suspicions up until that point.

"Any particular reason?" Mom asked, still eerily calm.

But I knew what she was doing. She wanted to figure out how many more lies she could get away with tonight.

"I saw everything," I spat, springing to my feet. The movement was a little wobbly seeing as how the edges of my vision were still blurred from losing consciousness, but I made sure to keep my gaze focused on Mom and Grams.

Herman, apparently sensing the drama that was about to unfold, pranced into the kitchen and leapt up onto the table to press himself into Grams' side, purring softly. Grams reached out an absentminded hand and ran it along his back gently.

"How old is that cat?" I demanded suddenly.

Mom and Grams looked down at Herman, then back at me.

"The... cat," Grams repeated.

"Yes, the cat," I replied. "Is that not what he is? Are you going to tell me we're aliens, too?"

"Oh my goodness we are not aliens!" Mom guffawed. "Don't be ridiculous, babe."

"Uh-uh." I shook my head vehemently. "I am not the ridiculous one. You wanna know what's ridiculous? The fact that you've been lying to me for forty years. What's your number one rule, Mom?"

Elle McCarthy's eyes went so wide, she might as well have been a character in a cartoon. Her mouth plopped open, but she managed to snap it closed quickly and shake her head.

"Rules don't apply to moms, remember?" She crooned, calling back to what she used to tell me as a child.

"That doesn't work anymore," I replied evenly. "The rules have completely gone out the window, clearly! I mean, who keeps secrets like this? Secrets. I don't even know what these secrets are! I mean, are we aliens, or like, some sort of creatures from a parallel dimension, or did we pop out of a TV show and just appear in this realm? So many possibilities. So many lies. So many things have been happening, and I couldn't explain them. But now I can! I think. I don't know. Maybe I can't. Like the flight attendant. And the tire. Ooh, I hope that stupid woman with her stupid Tesla got stranded on the side of the road for hours!"

I have this horrible tic, see, when I get stressed. Well, maybe it's not a tic so much as a really poor coping mechanism. Kenneth used to call it my "crazy time," because when I'd have a particularly stressful case, I'd pace around the living room for hours and hours, talking aloud to myself and trying to work out all of the kinks in the situation.

Without even realizing it, that was exactly what I was doing now. It wasn't until I ran straight into one of the kitchen chairs and probably bruised my hip that I realized I wasn't even talking to Mom and Grams anymore. I was sort of talking *at* them.

The two of them were the picture of calm, though, as they watched me make an insane attempt to turn a freak show of a situation into something semi-normal.

An impossible task.

I sucked in a deep breath and turned to them, mustering up as much calm as I possibly could.

"You done?" Mom asked with a quirked eyebrow.

"Yes," I sighed. "All done."

"Sit down." She pointed to the chair in front of me.

"No, it's fine," I shook my head, even though my legs were a little wobbly. But I was filled with this juvenile determination to do the exact opposite of everything my mom wanted.

"Sit, before you faint again," Grams ordered,

her voice stern.

"Okay, I'm sitting," I put my hands up in defense, and plopped my butt in the chair.

A pregnant pause filled the room. The kind of tense silence you can actually hear, as if the atoms themselves are buzzing with stress and anxiety.

"We're witches," Mom finally said.

It was confirmation of something I'd already hypothesized. But that didn't make it any less preposterous when she finally said it.

And the *way* she said it. With such important finality, as if she'd been gearing up for this conversation for years.

Which, I supposed she must have been, if she'd been hiding magic from me this entire time.

I couldn't even look at them in that moment. The betrayal I felt was like a rock twisting and growing inside my stomach, pressing on my lungs and making it nearly impossible to breathe. It made me want to puke or punch something all at once.

I dropped my face into my hands and stared down at the wooden table, taking note of every craggy little dent in its surface. Bruises from a long life of sitting in our kitchen, dealing with two growing girls and countless visitors, endless visits from teenagers who didn't know the meaning of the word "antique," and, apparently, whatever sort of witchy magic Mom and Grams had been cooking up in here for the last... who knew how long.

I guess my silence must have started to scare Mom, because I felt her kneel down next to me and put her hand flat on my back, rubbing it up and down like she always did when I was this upset.

Except, for the first time in my life, my own mother was the one who had caused this immeasurable ache in my heart.

"Say something, Shannon, please," she murmured.

For a moment, I couldn't. There was a lump in my throat the size of Antarctica, and I was afraid that if I opened my mouth, all that would come out would be an uncontrollable torrent of tears and snot.

Herman, in a very uncharacteristic move, pranced across the table and nuzzled the top of my head, purring the whole way.

"That's a good familiar," Grams murmured behind me, almost to herself.

"Familiar?" I mumbled curiously. My head snapped up, and I was once again reminded that I had about a thousand million questions to ask them, the first of which started with "How," and ended with "is that freaking cat still alive?"

"Yes," Grams nodded. "Not every witch has them, of course. Your mother doesn't. But some of us do."

"But shouldn't he have, like, died, or something?" I asked.

Herman, outraged by the very thought of his death, leapt away from me with an angry hiss.

"No," Grams replied. "A familiar dies with his witch. So, if I live to be two hundred and three, so will Herman."

"We're not immortal, are we?" I demanded. Suddenly, the very thought of an eternity in this miserable human world struck me as the most horrendous thing that could possibly happen.

"No, that's not our clan," Mom responded. "Look, baby girl, it has been a long night, and I'm sure you have more questions—"

"Try a thousand," I interjected.

"Right," she nodded. "But don't you think it would be better if we sat down and had a chat about all of this when the sun is out and our brains are clear?"

I narrowed my eyes as I tried to decipher where the hidden agenda was in her words, but I couldn't find one.

I did need time to come up with all of my questions, and to be able to sort my thought into something more than what I currently expected to be a barrage of accusations and demands. That probably wasn't the best way to approach this situation.

The truth of the matter was that I had a lot to learn, and I needed time to learn it all. Plus, the conversation would probably be a lot more fruitful if my mom and I didn't butt heads the entire way.

"Alright," I relented. "Sleep. But I expect both of you to be up at the crack of dawn and ready with forty years' worth of answers, got it?"

Mom and Grams nodded, if a little hesitantly, and I marched myself right out of that kitchen and went into my bedroom.

But I didn't sleep a wink. Instead, I spent the next five hours coming up with a list of questions to ask them. It might have been a little--okay, a lot--Type A of me, but I couldn't help it. When my brain felt so disorganized I was worried it might explode, the best way for me to deal with it had always been to put my thoughts down on paper.

And boy, did I have a lot of those.

9

THE NEXT MORNING felt like Christmas. That is, it would have, if Christmas was dark, and scary, and full of secrets and lies.

Maybe Christmas was actually a bad analogy.

But I sure as heck sat next to my door that morning and waited until I heard the familiar clomp of my mother's feet charging down the hall, headed for the kitchen and her coffee, which was pretty much like liquid gold to her in the mornings. A few seconds later, I heard Grams' little pitter patter as she also headed toward the kitchen, a lot more gracefully than her daughter did.

"Okay, Shannon, this is it," I told myself,

sucking in a breath as I stared down at the image in the mirror.

The face was familiar, but that was the only thing I still recognized about myself. There were dark circles under my eyes, ones that I would have never allowed to exist as the Boston D.A. My usually styled and smooth hair had turned into a frizzy, curly mess that resembled my mother's head full of crazy hair, and there was a darkness in my green eyes that almost scared me.

Not an evil darkness, of course. More like one of determination and... well, I wasn't quite sure what else was there. All I knew was that my own eyes were unfamiliar to me.

My inner poet wanted to make some grand statement about how that look in my eyes was reflective of my inner change and turmoil, of the secret darkness I'd kept hidden inside of me for so long.

Was magic dark? Did my newfound status as something out of a children's fairytale mean that I was also evil, like the Queen in *Snow White*, or Ursula in *The Little Mermaid*?

Mom and Grams certainly didn't strike me as evil. They didn't even like to kill the spiders that wandered into the house to get out of the Portland rain. And I definitely couldn't say that the patrons of Magic for Real seemed like they had any sort of vile plots brewing in their minds.

Or at least, I wouldn't have said that as a teenager. After seeing the number of acrylic-nailed, kale-drinking, copy-and-paste blondes that had come into the store over the last few days, I was absolutely sure at least a few of them were trying to cast a spell or two on their high school nemesis.

But did that make them evil?

It was too much to think about on an empty stomach. I shook my head, fluffed my hair to attempt to get some sort of order back into my life, and went downstairs to get all of my questions answered.

"Good morning sunshine!" Mom grinned at me as she handed me a cup of coffee.

"You don't talk in the morning," I pointed out gruffly.

That was possibly the understatement of the century. Usually, if anyone so much as breathed too close to Elle McCarthy before ten a.m., they'd find themselves with a wad of gum in their hair and rocks in their boots before they could even apologize.

"I'm trying something new," she asserted,

drifting back across the kitchen to take a seat at the table.

I took a suspicious sip of my coffee before I stopped and spit out the warm, comforting liquid.

"You haven't drugged this or anything, right?" I demanded. "Added some sort of memory potion so I forget all about witches and magic?"

"Of course not!" Mom gasped.

"Child, we have never lied to you about magic," Grams said seriously. "We've always told you that magic existed. It was you who chose not to believe in it."

"You never told me I was a witch!" I exclaimed indignantly. "There's a pretty big difference between: 'oh, yep, this rock has magical energy,' and 'by the way, you happen to come from a line of creatures born out of myth and legend.'"

"Well, we were expecting you to get your powers, just like the rest of us," Mom retorted. "And when you didn't get your magic, I figured it might be best to let you stay in the dark, so you didn't feel so badly about yourself. Besides, you were off in Boston going to college, and then you met Kenneth, and you seemed so happy with him that I didn't want to ruin it."

"Oh, now you care about my relationship with

Kenneth?" I snapped. "You never liked him. You should have jumped at the chance to bring me back home."

"Look, Shannon, contrary to what you might believe, I really wanted you to be happy with him," Mom sighed. "But I also know that this family doesn't exactly mix well with the opposite gender, and I wanted to make sure you were prepared for that."

Intense hurt flooded her emerald green eyes, and the biting words that had leapt to my tongue soon fell away. I couldn't argue with my mom when she looked at me like that.

For the first time since I'd met Kenneth, I realized that my mom didn't actually hate him. She was serious.

She knew how it was going to end before I ever did, and she just didn't want me to get hurt. As angry as I was about all the lies and deception, that realization tugged at my heartstrings. Underneath it all, she was still my mom, and she just wanted what was best for me.

Only, right now, we heavily disagreed on just what that was.

"Okay," I sighed. "I get it. Not completely, but... it's okay."

"Thank you." Mom offered me a slightly watery smile. She bit her lip nervously and sucked in a breath.

To be honest, it kind of shocked me. My mom wasn't ever a nervous person. She was bold and brash, and as annoying as it could be, it was also one of the things I admired most about her. So the worried energy that flowed from her in droves made my heart pound in my chest.

This wasn't what I wanted. I didn't want my mom to feel terrified to even talk to me. But, at the same time, the betrayal I still felt ran deep.

"Well, what do you want to know?" Grams broke the silence by asking.

"Um, everything?" I laughed lightly. "What's this whole thing with getting powers at twenty-one about?"

"That's a McCarthy clan curse," Mom explained. "Or gift, depending on how you want to look at it. Each clan has their own little... quirk, let's say. In our family, only the women possess magic, and they don't come into their powers until they're twenty-one years of age."

"So how come I didn't get my powers then?"

To be honest, now that this whole magic thing was out in the open, I was a little bit hurt that I hadn't gotten my magic on time.

Assuming, of course, that whatever was going

on with me was, in fact, magic, and not just some sort of random coincidence.

"I'm not sure," Grams sighed. "We waited and waited, hoping you'd call us up one day and say that something strange had happened, and then you'd finally believe in all of the things we'd been telling you since you were a child, but you didn't. And then your twenty second birthday came and went, and your twenty third..."

Grams trailed off as she thought about all of the years she'd spent waiting for me to grow into my powers. A twang of hurt twisted in my stomach at the look in her eyes. I felt like I'd disappointed her without even meaning to, like I hadn't lived up to the unspoken expectation placed upon me at birth.

"I decided it was better you didn't know," Mom said when it became clear Grams was lost in her thoughts. "I thought that, maybe, you could live a normal life. Being a witch isn't exactly easy."

"Yeah, I think I'm figuring that out," I mumbled, a little annoyed about all of the weird occurrences that kept happening to me. At least now I could put my finger on their cause.

"What do you mean?" Mom asked.

I looked back up at her, and saw that confusion had filled her green eyes.

"I thought you knew I've been doing magic," I responded. "Well, not 'doing,' exactly. None of it's been intentional. But I made the flight attendant let me on the plane, even though I was terribly late. And I popped this lady's tire out just with my mind."

"You got your powers?" Grams gasped. "Now? After all this time?"

Yet again, I was feeling like the odd man out.

"Yeah," I responded hesitantly. "Is that super weird? I can't be the only late bloomer in the family. I even got my period late."

Fifteen, to be exact. I'd ended up lying about my monthly visitor the entirety of my freshman year of high school.

Once again, Mom and Grams shared a look.

"Hey!" I interrupted their silent conversation. "I thought we were done with the looks now that I'm in on the whole witch thing?"

"What, exactly, has been happening to you?" Mom asked carefully. She even pushed her coffee mug away from her as she listened to my answer. That was how I knew this was serious.

"I mean, not much," I shrugged. "I haven't blown anyone up, or anything. But there was the tire thing, and the flight attendant, like I mentioned. And the moving boxes seemed to pack themselves. I don't even remember doing those. Mostly, though, it was the vision I had last night that sealed the de—"

"VISION?" Grams shrieked, standing up so freaking fast she knocked her mug full of her morning tea over.

"Jesus!" I gasped as the boiling liquid rapidly made its way across the table toward me. I snatched a dish towel from the rack behind me and mopped it up before any of the scorching liquid could cause permanent damage.

"Mama, calm down!" my mother hollered.

Instantly, Grams plopped back down in her seat, and then proceeded to stare at her hands and mutter something that was completely incoherent.

"What is going on?" I was pleading with them at this point. It felt like, every time I stepped one inch closer to the truth, I was pushed an entire foot and a half backward.

"It's nothing," my mom said quickly.

"It is so clearly not nothing!" I challenged. "You've already told me this much. What is it about the vision that freaked you out? Do you want to know what I saw?"

"NO!" My mom roared. The abruptness of her outburst scared me so badly that I instantly slammed my mouth shut. Mom took in a deep, steadying breath and forced herself to calm down. "I'm sorry. Just... don't ever speak of this vision again, alright? To *anybody.*"

Her expression was pleading. And pleading was not a look Elle McCarthy wore, well, ever.

"Fine," I hissed. "I won't talk to anyone. Including the two of you. This house is full of nothing but lies and deceit, and I want absolutely nothing to do with it."

I leapt from my chair, grabbed my purse from the rack, and sprinted toward the door.

"Shannon, wait!" My mom called after me, but I didn't even bother to slow down in the slightest.

I was tired of the lies. I was being lied to in Boston, and it had ruined my marriage. So I'd come home, to the place I'd thought I would be safe, so that I could start all over again, and build a life from the ground up.

But even my new foundation had been seeded with swindling, tricks, and deceit.

10

I DIDN'T EVEN KNOW where my feet were carrying me until I arrived. And, at that point, I was standing outside of Rockstar Coffee, heaving.

I'd run there. I was vaguely aware of that fact. It probably hadn't helped the image of disarray I'd had going on when I looked in the mirror that morning, but I couldn't bring myself to care. I didn't normally step out in public looking anything less than put together, but, hell, if the rest of my life had crumbled to dust, I might as well allow my appearance to do so as well.

As my bad luck would have it, I was once again greeted by the pimple faced, judgey cashier when I walked into Rockstar Coffee. The place was mostly empty, seeing as it was barely seven a.m. on a chilly Portland Saturday, but I liked it that way. I needed some me time, away from literally everyone else in the world.

"Let me guess," the kid sighed as I approached, "dark roast coffee. Cream and sugar. Nothing else."

I was about to nod when I started to think about it.

Everything else in my life seemed to be going to hell? So why not live a little and try something outside of my usually perfectly formed box.

"You know what, kid? Give me one of those zebra mocha things, and a chocolate croissant."

The kid raised an eyebrow and stared at me for a moment, trying to figure out if this was some sort of prank. After about thirty seconds, he must have decided that I was, in fact, serious, because he shrugged and typed it into the computer.

"ZEBRA MOCHA AND A CHOCOLATE CROISSANT!" He hollered over his shoulder, even louder than the last time I'd been in, if that was even possible. Then, he turned back to me and gave me the total. "Eleven oh two."

This time, I didn't even blink. I'd started to get used to the outrageous prices here in the new

Portland. As far as I was concerned, hipster was just a fancy way of saying expensive.

I handed over my card, let him ring me up, and then sat down in the little, isolated table while I waited for my breakfast. If I could even call it that. The meal was so full of sugar I wasn't sure it counted.

In fact, I told myself that nothing I ate for the rest of the day counted. I wouldn't worry about calories, or sugar, or how much of my daily iron intake was in whatever food I decided to stuff in my mouth. No, today was purely about eating my feelings.

Which I did, as soon as the croissant showed up at my table. I stuffed half the thing into my mouth at once and closed my eyes as I felt the warm deliciousness melt across my tongue. It was as if the silky smooth chocolate was a temporary cure for all of my pain. For just a few seconds, I could forget that my life had turned into an absolute mess quicker than I could have blinked.

In fact, I could almost delude myself into believing I was back in Boston, enjoying a nice treat the morning before I had to work a hard case. As soon as the day was over, I'd head to my perfect home, where my husband would be waiting with a bottle of red wine and the newest Marvel movie on our giant, flatscreen TV.

"Are you eating that food or having sex with it?"

Hunter.

I'd recognize his voice anywhere, especially when it was booming down from right above me like some sort of God.

Slowly, I opened one eye and looked up at him.

"What's it to you?" I demanded. "We weren't supposed to meet today."

"I'm not meeting you," he laughed. "I just happened to decide it was a good day for a coffee, walked into my new favorite coffee shop, and, lo and behold, here you are. Looking like you're about to become one with the back half of a chocolate croissant."

"It's my comfort food," I replied defensively, not even aware that I was sharing personal information with a virtual stranger.

His eyes were just so... magnificent. It was like those steely gray balls in his head absorbed every rational thought I could possibly have, and I was left with a big old pile of goop for brains.

"Your comfort food," he repeated, as his bushy

brown eyebrows knitted together. "Something's wrong."

It was a statement, and not a question.

For the first time since I met him, which wasn't actually all that long ago, I saw what seemed to be genuine compassion in his eyes. But then, a cloud floated over them, and they turned almost...

Calculating?

It was a weird thing to see in this man's eyes. I didn't know him all that well, but he didn't really strike me as the calculating type.

For a split second, I wondered if he was a witch, too. Maybe he could sense my powers, or something sort of magical and cool like that. But if he could, why hadn't he said anything to me? Especially since we'd already been talking about the case a bit.

"Nothing's wrong." I decided denial was my best path and shook my head in a way that was meant to be discouraging.

"Nope, you're lying." Hunter cracked a smile at me.

"I, uh..." I was trying to say no, that I was telling the truth. But I'd never been a very good liar, even as a child. That was probably why it was my job to prosecute the liars.

"Get up," Hunter instructed suddenly.

"What?"

"Get. Up," he replied with a dopey, boyish grin. "The best cure for sadness is to get up on your feet and move about. Let's go, Shannon."

"I don't want to move about," I whined, almost like a child. "I want to sit right here and mope."

"Not gonna happen."

Before I could protest any further, I was being unceremoniously yanked out of my chair. It was all I could do to grab the last half of my croissant and the mocha, which I'd had the foresight to put in a to go cup, before I was nearly dragged out of the coffee shop.

"Hunter, where are we going?" I was trying to make my voice sound demanding but, to my utter dismay, I couldn't keep the hint of excitement out of my tone.

So sue me. Hunter was good looking, and there was something about him that just drew me in--not that I'd ever act on it--and it was a little bit exciting to have a man like that just decide he wanted to spend time with me so spontaneously.

Kenneth was never spontaneous. He used to plan his entire day down to the minute, and he'd charge one of his poor clerks with making sure he kept to the schedule. That was probably why I married him. He was just as neurotic as I was.

But Hunter was the exact opposite of neurotic. Hunter was instinctive. He moved like an animal, and made decisions on the fly, and thought with his gut instead of his head.

I could tell those instincts were what made him a good P.I., even if he wouldn't let me see it yet.

"Okay, sit," Hunter ordered.

I'd been so entrenched in the depths of my thoughts that I hadn't even realized he'd dragged me all the way out to the middle of the park, next to the duck pond, where all the kids were playing around on the grass. He pointed to an old, wooden bench that had probably been around since before my grandmother had even arrived in Portland, before he sat down himself.

"Alright," I sat down hesitantly, still a little unsure as to why he'd taken a sudden interest in me. "What's the deal with this bench?"

"It's just nice," he shrugged. "I like to come out here when I'm really caught up in the case, trying to figure everything out but not getting anywhere."

"And what makes you think I'm trying to figure something out?" I demanded.

Hunter turned to me and gave me a once over, a half smile lighting up his face.

"You're not?" He grinned.

"Fine," I sighed. "I am trying to figure something out. It's…"

Well, I couldn't exactly tell him the truth, now could I? I caught myself before I dumped an entire insane asylum's worth of crazy right into his lap. Sure, we'd been talking about the murders, but neither one of us had thought they'd had anything to do with the occult. Now, obviously, I knew that wasn't at all true, but what would Hunter think if I told him that?

He'd probably write me off as a total nutball, and then I'd be down my only friend. If we even were friends, after all.

"What is it?" He prompted.

"I just found out my family's been hiding this big secret from me," I replied. I could at least tell him that much. "And they're still lying to me about other stuff, even after I caught them in the first lie. I'm just starting to feel like I don't even have solid ground to stand on anymore, like everything I thought I knew about myself just disappeared, just like that."

I snapped my fingers for emphasis. Red hot tears stung my eyes, and I forced myself to stare at the duck pond so Hunter couldn't see me crying. I watched as a pristine, pure white duck let out a loud quack, and then tipped its whole body forward to dive for bugs and fish.

"What were they lying to you about?" Hunter asked.

His tone was open and honest. I think I was about to tell him, too, disregarding all reason and logic, until I saw the expression in his eyes.

There it was again. That darkness I'd seen before, the one I couldn't totally place.

So as much as my heart wanted to spill my new, darkest secret to this near total stranger, I felt myself pulling back, a little wary of this sometimes-malicious glint that would enter Hunter's eyes.

At the same time, though, something deep within me told me I could trust him. It was strange, almost like a whisper of my intuition, like there was some inner being who actually spoke to me and told me that Hunter was one of the good guys, that he was on my side.

I hoped that was true.

"Just family stuff." I waved my hands in the air, as if it was normal family stuff, like my brother was actually my father, or some other sort of soap opera-esque thing.

Not that I had a brother. Or a father.

"Hmm." Hunter nodded. "Well, that sounds awful. I've got to go."

He stood up so abruptly he nearly knocked over my half empty coffee cup.

"Wait, what?" I demanded. "Why do you have to go?"

"I've got a case to solve," he shrugged.

"So do I," I replied.

At this point, I really did. Someone was targeting witches in this town, which meant that my mom and Grams were in danger.

And so was I.

"No, you don't," Hunter shook his head. "I work alone."

"Really? Because you seemed awfully freaking interested in me when I was looking over those cold cases."

"I just wanted another perspective," Hunter hedged, but it didn't feel like the truth to me.

"Come on," I pleaded. "I need to get my mind off of family secrets, just for an hour or two. Let me help you."

It wasn't a *total* lie. Trying to solve these murders would absolutely take my mind off the fact that everyone I'd ever trusted seemed to find it fitting to lie right to my face for lengthy periods of time.

Hunter had already started down the path, shaking his head in annoyance. So I ran after him.

I'd always been persistent, and today was no different.

"You're going to follow me until I say yes, aren't you?" Hunter sighed.

"Yep." I nodded. "So you might as well just give in now."

"Fine," he replied begrudgingly. "But if you get in my way, I maintain the right to send you home at any moment."

I didn't reply. He could sure as hell try to send me home, but I wouldn't be going.

11

I FOLLOWED Hunter all the way back to his apartment, about a mile and a half away from Rockstar Coffee.

To my absolute chagrin, I was nearly huffing and puffing by the time we got there, while he was breathing deep and meditatively, like the long walk up and down the hills of Portland was no skin off of his back.

Exercise and McCarthy women didn't exactly mix too well. Come to think of it, McCarthy women didn't mix well with an awful lot of things.

"It's…nice."

I struggled to find a better description for the tiny apartment Hunter led me to. Nice was just about the best I could do, considering the place looked like nobody even lived there.

It was one of those newfangled studio apartments, the one landlords dubbed "bachelor pads," so they could get away without having to use the words "no kitchen" in the description.

In fact, there was pretty much nothing but a sink and a hot plate against the far right wall, a mattress pushed up against the left, and a tiny little bathroom next to the doorway that had a toilet, sink, and standing shower.

Look, I'm not a super fancy woman. Sure, I liked my Louboutins and my pressed skirts, but I'd grown up in a tiny, messy little house. But I drew the line at a kitchenless shoebox apartment with no bed.

"Did you know your nose crinkles when you lie?" Hunter asked suddenly.

"What? No it doesn't!" I actually pulled out my phone so I could look at myself in the reflection of the black screen.

"It does," Hunter replied, his gray eyes dancing with mirth. "Just at the top here."

He tapped the bridge of his nose, right where it met his forehead, to indicate where my apparent tell was.

"Okay, Mr. Lie Detector," I laughed. "Let's just get down to business, huh? What have you got?"

"You're bossy."

"I'm used to being in charge," I shrugged.

"Take a seat." He pointed at the mattress on the floor.

Carefully, I sat right on the very edge, avoiding any part that may have touched... God only knew what Hunter did in that bed.

The P.I. pulled out a stack of papers from the single yellow filing cabinet in the room and plopped them at my feet. Before I could reach for them, though, one of his hands shot out and caught mine.

"I have a question for you first," he stated seriously.

Those steely gray eyes bored into my own and sent my heart into an annoying flutter.

"What?" I asked, a little breathlessly.

"How'd you know about the bag of herbs?"

Crap.

I'd completely forgotten that, in my terrified haze after that crazy vision the night before, I'd texted the only person who would have known anything about the case.

Hunter.

And in doing so, could have given myself away. But he didn't believe in magic, right?

My mind raced to find a plausible cover up, and I finally stumbled on one that I'd used plenty of times before, when I was trying to drag a confession out of a criminal.

"I overheard some of the women talking about it at my family's shop," I replied. "Buncha crazy ladies. They think someone's targeting witches."

Okay, I admit, it was a double-edged move. I wanted to cover my tracks while also digging for information that I didn't think Hunter would just offer up to me.

I watched him closely, and he knew it, because he kept his features smooth and his reaction even.

"Interesting," he frowned. "What else did they say?"

"Uhhhhh," I drew out the sound to attempt to give myself a little more time to think of a plausible response that would also get me a little bit closer to the information I needed. "All the witches seem to be shopping at Magic for Real. My Grams owns it. She's a little crazy."

I was sure as hell not about to tell him that she was the one who was worried.

"Yep," Hunter nodded. "Well, whoever you

overheard is right. The killer's targeting a coven of witches, just like they did last time."

I think my jaw hit the floor. I was absolutely certain that when I woke up in the morning, I'd find a big, long, purple bruise on the underside of my jaw, right where it smacked down on the hard laminate flooring of Hunter's apartment.

"A coven?" I breathed reflexively.

Thousands of thoughts swirled through my head, so many that I found it nearly impossible to keep track of them all.

First, there was the fact that Hunter actually believed in magic and witches. And then, on top of that, that this killer was targeting us. And then, on top of *that*, the fact that the killer wanted an entire coven dead.

"That's what I said," he nodded. "They got twelve last time. One short of thirteen. And whoever's doing it this time is going for the same number."

"You don't think it's the same person?" I prodded.

"Not likely," Hunter looked at me. "What, do you not believe in magic?"

Here was the time to make a decision. If I said I did, he might be able to figure out my secret. I didn't know how, but the man was smart. But, on the flip side, if I said no, he might stop working with me, and then I'd be out of luck when it came to this case. I didn't have any resources here in Portland, so I needed to rely on Hunter to get all of the information for me.

"I guess I've never thought about it." That seemed like a good, diplomatic, rational answer. One that wouldn't give my secrets away and, at the same time, wouldn't make Hunter want to toss me out of his apartment.

"You are a strange one, Shannon McCarthy," he chuckled.

"What makes you say that?" I demanded indignantly. I didn't like being called strange. It reminded me too much of being a kid and having to explain why my house was covered in all sorts of occult items.

"You just... are."

He wasn't trying to be insulting, I could tell by his tone. He sounded more surprised than anything else, which only served to confuse me. I didn't understand this man. He ran hot and cold faster than a rich person's sink could flip from one temperature to the next. One minute, I felt like I was this massive annoyance, and the next, it seemed like he was rather glad to have my company.

"Alright, fine, so say they're witches," I announced, rather artfully changing the subject. "What sort of belief systems do they hold? What's their deal?"

"Well, first, I don't think they call it a 'deal,'" he chuckled. He yanked a piece of paper from one of the files and handed it to me. "See this? It's an account from Muriel's best friend. Her name's Theodosia Arlington. She owns some bookstore here in town... Books Are Friends, I think it's called."

The world exploded around me in that moment. Either that, or I was having a panic attack. Books Are Friends was the store I'd wandered into, the one where the candle flames had grown to impossible heights, and where that woman felt like something was off about my energy. I assumed she was the owner.

Which meant she and Muriel were best friends, and it wasn't too much of a stretch to think they were in the same coven. The same one Mom and Grams were in, if those other ten pictures were any indicator.

I brought myself back down to earth and focused on the paper in my hands so Hunter didn't see the little freakout I'd just had.

"This is her testimony?" I asked, staring at the

page in my hands. "How the hell did you get the cops to hand this over?"

"I can be very persuasive," Hunter shrugged. "Look, here's the part where Theodosia says they were a coven. And look at the other two names listed."

"Ernestine Lockwood and Honey Biggs," I breathed. "They were all in the same one."

Of course, I'd already known this. But Theodosia's statement simply confirmed my hypothesis.

I had to find this bastard before he found my family. There was no way I was letting them die, even if they were liars and I reserved the right to hold a grudge against them for the rest of my life.

"Precisely," Hunter nodded. "Believe it or not, they're being targeted. The only problem is, Theodosia wouldn't give up the names of the other nine. So we have no way of knowing who their next victim is."

"So, what, they got together and did spells and stuff?" I pressed him.

To be totally honest, I was using Hunter as my own personal magic Google right then. I couldn't bear the thought of asking Mom and Grams anything, since it seemed every question I brought up was shut down immediately. Like my question about the vision.

"Something like that," Hunter nodded.

"And I bet they see the future, too," I laughed, making an attempt to cover my very serious question with a joke.

But my newfound partner in crime found absolutely nothing funny about that.

"No," he barked. "They're not psychic. That's a fae power."

No matter how hard I tried, my poker face did not want to stay the moment he said those words.

"A fae power?" I choked. "As in... fairies, and whatnot? Like *The Lord of the Rings*?"

My voice was so high pitched I probably could have called a dog over.

"Not quite. More like, Shakespearean beings whose only intentions are, well, evil."

"Oh, good." I gulped audibly. So now, not only was I a witch, but I had some sort of weird fae power that meant... Well, I didn't exactly know what it meant. But I knew who could give me some answers.

And they shared my last name.

"I have to go." I stood abruptly, knocking the papers from my lap and scattering them all across Hunter's bare floor. I should have stayed to pick them up, since that was the polite thing to do, but I couldn't bring myself to hang around any longer knowing that I was a fae. Or had a fae power. Or... I didn't even know.

"But we barely got started looking into this," Hunter protested. "There's still so much shit to talk about."

"Another time," I insisted. "I just remembered that I have to go and do something."

"Do what?"

Boy, he was as persistent as I was. I could see why it annoyed him so much now.

"Doesn't matter," I snapped, a little more rudely than I intended. "I just have to go, okay? Have a good afternoon."

I couldn't leave on a completely rude note. Even so, I spun out of Hunter's apartment faster than a spider spins a web, feeling the whole time like I was drowning in an empty swimming pool.

I had a fae power. So what did that mean?

1 2

I ONLY MADE it halfway down the block before I had to lean over a trash can so I could completely puke my guts out.

Normally, I'm not a puking person. In fact, I think the last time I threw up, I was still in law school, and had given myself the worst hangover known to man. Suffice it to say, food hadn't come up the wrong way in over a decade.

But this was a whole lot worse than the world's most terrible hangover. This was... Shakespearean?

Actually, no. I didn't think that even Shakespeare was enough of a genius to dream up this fantastic level of absolute craziness.

By the time I'd finished puking my guts out, I counted at least two rude looks from strangers, and one homeless guy who seemed a little bit too interested in what I had for breakfast.

But, in true Shannon fashion, I stood up straight, shook out my hair, and walked on down the street with my head held high.

I turned into the gravel driveway of the familiar cottage house about ten minutes later.

The outside was still the same as it had been when I was a kid. But now, it was as if I was seeing everything with a brand new set of eyes. The line of tiny stone gargoyles that guarded the porch suddenly had a whole new meaning. The rocks scattered among the herbs were no longer just pretty things to look at, but a symbol of energy and magic.

And then there was the herbs themselves, the strange plants that I'd explained away to visiting friends and boyfriends, and even to myself. My family just had a weird obsession with different types of plants. After all, who would want to live in a house with the same boring grass and oak trees that everyone else had?

Not me, that's for sure.

Now, though, boring seemed like it would have been wonderful compared to the twisted maze of secrets and lies my life had become.

I stepped up to the old door, stuck my key in the lock, and swung it wide open to reveal the familiar, and yet strange, house.

Just as the items in the front yard had, the clutter in Grams' house took on a whole new level of meaning. The charm that hung over the front door to ward off fairies and their ilk now twisted my stomach, and the candles on the mantle of the fireplace, made of beeswax and filled with all sorts of strange herbs, seemed to mock me.

If I was fae, how come the charms didn't ward me off? How come the magic of the candles hadn't thrown me out of the house? I couldn't be fae. It had to be a coincidence. The vision must have been some sort of random dream I'd had that just so happened to be real. Mom and Grams would have some sort of explanation.

I hoped.

I was still in the doorway, taking everything in, when Mom came around the corner, from the kitchen. She froze when she saw me, and stared at me nervously, waiting for me to make the first move.

For a long moment, I couldn't find words. I just stood there looking at her, replaying every single memory we'd had together. Every moment I felt like she was hiding something, every time I caught her looking at me longingly, like she wished I was something more.

I was starting to understand those small, seemingly insignificant moments now. I used to brush them off, thinking that everyone had those problems with their mother.

But I was wrong. Nobody did but me. As much as I used to long for a life full of extraordinary wonder, in that moment I would have given everything I had for the boring, mundane normalcy everyone else possessed.

"I'm still mad," I finally said, breaking the silence abruptly.

Mom's eyes filled with tears that never fell.

"I'd expect nothing less," she replied, cracking a half-hearted smile and trying to turn it into a joke.

"You lied to me." Again, I stated the obvious, but they were words that I felt needed to be said.

"Would it help if I got down on my knees and pleaded for your forgiveness?" Mom asked jokingly.

"Maybe," I responded, faking as if I begrudged the thought. In truth, an apology seemed nice. It didn't have to be dramatic.

And right as I had that thought, Elle Mc-Carthy dropped to her knees and scooched over to me, pretending like she was performing in front of a massive audience instead of just me.

"I'm sorry!" She wailed, full of enough melodrama to earn her a spot on *The Young and the Restless*. "I shouldn't have lied to you, my darling daughter. I knew it was wrong, and yet I did it anyway. I am a terrible, horrible mother who simply wanted you to live your best, safest life. How dare I!"

At that point, my mom was right in front of me, with her wrist draped over her forehead like a damsel in distress in some old movie. She opened one eye and peeked out at me from underneath her arm to gauge my reaction.

"I suppose that's enough," I sighed sarcastically.

"Good, because my knees ain't exactly what they used to be." Mom laughed as she stood up. Her chuckling quickly turned serious as she looked right into my eyes. "I really am sorry, though, baby. I thought it was the right move at the time, and as soon as I was old enough, and wise enough, to think that maybe it wasn't… it was too late, Shan. You would have either been just as mad as you are now, or you would have thought we were bonkers."

"Let's get one thing straight--I definitely think you're bonkers," I giggled. "But you're my bonkers, and I love you."

That was all it took for Mom to wrap me up in her signature bear hug, squeezing the life out of me with each passing second. I let her have her fun for a few moments, but when I started to feel like I might pass out for the second time today, I realized it was probably best to get out of her stranglehold.

"Mom... Can't breathe," I gasped.

"Right, sorry," she sprang backward.

"So, does this mean you forgive your old grandma, too?" Grams called from down the hall.

"Of course it does," I laughed, and walked over to her. "But the two of you have some serious explaining to do."

Instantly, the mood in the room darkened, and Mom and Grams shared that damn look with each other.

"No. Uh-uh," I chopped my hand through the air between them, metaphorically signaling the end to those looks. "I'm in on this, now. You have to talk to me just as much as you talk to each other. And right now, I need all the answers you have to give."

"Shan," Mom started diplomatically. "How about we just take a day, take a breath, and let everything settle down before we dive deeper into our hairy family history, hmm?"

"Nope, not cutting it, lady," I replied. "I know having a vision is a fae power, and not a witch one. So how come I had one?"

There was a moment of silence as the two of them considered how much I already knew. I almost thought they might stand their ground like the stubborn mules they loved to be but, thankfully, they didn't.

"I'll make some tea," Grams sighed.

"And I'll get the whiskey," Mom added.

Five minutes later, we were steeping piping hot cups of black tea with a couple shots of whiskey in them and sitting at the kitchen table.

Which I was thinking of renaming. We did a hell of a lot more than eat at it.

"When I—" Grams started, at the exact same time that Mom said, "The thing is—"

"You start, Mama," My mom told Grams. "It's mostly your story, after all."

"It's all of our story," Grams replied.

I watched as my grandmother, a woman who

127

was normally so calm a bomb could have gone off and she wouldn't have so much as batted an eye, take a long sip of her whiskey infused tea. Finally, when she was satisfied she had enough alcohol to fill her system, she cleared her throat and looked back up at me.

"When I first came to Portland, I thought that I didn't need any of the typical conventions of life," she began. "In truth, I was outrunning all of that. I was outrunning magic, and the curse of our family. But I was also outrunning the expectations of the South. Even in the forties, Portland was progressive. Women here didn't need a man and babies to feel fulfilled. They had their friends, and jobs, and hobbies to fill them up. I met Auntie Deedee right off the bat, and the two of us had a wonderful little group of girlfriends. I was normal. And I thought that was all I needed."

I wanted to interject, but thought better of it at the last second. It was almost impossible for me to imagine the Grams I knew, who loved magic and witchcraft, wanting something normal.

I guess we had more in common than just our looks.

"But about a year after I moved, I started to feel this big ache in my heart," she continued, her eyes far away as she reminisced about the past. "I suspect it's the same one that caused you to flee Portland and run all the way to Boston. That ache that tells you there's something more out there in the world, and that you're missing it terribly. So, I cast a love spell, thinking I might just find a good, human man, and we'd raise some human babies, and I'd still be able to escape the curse of the McCarthy name."

"But life doesn't always work out the way you want it to," I laughed as I brought up one of Grams' absolute favorite sayings.

"Yes," she sighed. "The spell worked out, just as I'd hoped, and brought me the most wonderful man. His name was Laslow, and he was a fae."

Mom shifted uncomfortably in her chair when she heard her father's name. I recognized the feeling splayed across her face. I felt it quite often myself, whenever I thought about the father I'd never known.

"So, what happened to Laslow?" I murmured curiously.

Once again, Grams took a sip of her tea. An uncharacteristic tear rolled down her cheek and landed on the table, but she didn't seem to notice.

"He was, um, taken away from me," she replied, her voice thick with emotion. "The fae and the witches are not supposed to mix. And Laslow was punished because I called him to me with a spell."

Grams' voice broke at that last sentence, and Herman leapt up onto the table in front of her, meowing away in what I supposed was meant to be a calming manner.

"Oh, Mama, you can't blame yourself," Mom said, rubbing Grams' back gently. "It wasn't your fault. The rules are horrid and medieval, and anyone who's got any amount of sense would know that."

"That may be," Grams sighed, "but no matter how outdated we find them, they exist. And because of them, Laslow is... well, I don't even know what happened to him. And I doubt I ever will."

"Geez, I'm so sorry, Grams," I whispered. My heart ached for her. I couldn't imagine what it would have felt like to have Kenneth taken away from me for matters that were out of our control, especially at the height of our relationship, when I loved him more than anything else in the whole world.

"It's in the past," Grams replied, sucking in a breath and composing herself. "What matters now is the consequences that you and I must deal with."

"What do you mean?" I asked nervously.

"Shannon, darling, when your mom was a child, she started exhibiting some of the powers you have now. But, because she had not come into her witch magic yet, I was able to cast a spell meant to tear her away from her fae half. I am afraid that, in doing so, I may have simply locked it away within her. And when she was pregnant with you, those powers transferred to the fetus that was inside of her."

"So you're saying that... not only am I part fae, but I have extra fae powers because you, what, stored Mom's fae-ness in her uterus, or something?" I quirked a brow in confusion.

"No, Shannon, what I am saying is that you are both witch and fae," Grams replied. "But because I did not catch your fae powers in time, they have grown to astronomic proportions. Proportions that would terrify and anger many of the magical world."

"So why not just shut them down?" I asked. "Do to me what you did to Mom. Lock them away."

Even as I spoke, I could tell by the expressions on their faces that it was an impossibility.

"I was only able to lock your mother's fae powers away because I had the ring her father gave me," Grams said quietly. "The spell I used destroyed that ring. Shannon... I have no way to help you."

13

I FELT like I was in a surf tunnel, like in the aquarium. Or maybe one on the open oceans, like the types of tunnels pro surfers get caught up in and photographers snap those really cool pictures of. Then rich people buy them for astronomical amounts of money to frame on their wall and trick people into thinking that they're all athletic and whatnot.

The only problem was that I'd never been surfing. Hell, I don't even think I'd been to an aquarium since I was a tiny little kid. But I definitely knew what it felt like to be in one of those tunnels, with the water crashing down around me and swallowing me whole, because that was where I was right then.

"Shannon, breathe," Mom instructed, her voice tinged with worry.

It was only when I registered the fear in her voice that I realized I hadn't taken a breath in well over a minute. Gasping, I inhaled as much air as I possibly could, smelling the oils in the air, the way the sage smoke hung around me, meant to take the bad energy out of the house and sweep it off somewhere it couldn't harm anyone.

Clearly, it wasn't doing its job very well.

"Are you—" Mom started, but I put a hand up to silently signal for her not to ask. I don't know why, but just the thought of my mom trying to figure out if I was okay in that moment would have caused me to crumble and fall apart. That was the last thing I needed, or wanted, to do right then.

"I'll be fine." My voice was barely above a whisper. It was all I could muster, though. I didn't think my vocal cords were strong enough to handle anything louder at that moment.

Slowly, I stood up from the table, trying my best not to fall over and collapse. It would have made me feel weak to do so, and if there was one thing I prided myself on never being, it was weak. Weakness was for people who had it easy. It was for women who couldn't pull themselves together.

I wasn't weak.

I couldn't be weak. Because in a way, that would have felt like giving in.

"Shannon, we can figure something else out," Mom tried again. But out of the corner of my eye, I saw Grams shake her head, only once, but it was definitive.

There was no other way.

"We need something of your father's, Elle," she murmured. "Something that would recognize his DNA in Shannon. And that's..."

Grams voice trailed off, too thick with tears and emotion to really continue.

"Impossible, I know," Mom sighed.

I recognized that sigh. I'd probably done it a million times before, whenever I'd asked about my own father.

As I looked at my Mom and Grams sitting there at our old kitchen table, surrounded by a lifetime's worth of trinkets meant to enhance their magic and ward off evil, I couldn't take it any more.

Suddenly, they looked old to me. Frail, in a way. Like the secret of a lifetime had been lifted from their shoulders, and now it was all they could do to remain upright in their seats.

"I have to go." The words surprised even myself when they came out of my mouth. Mom's head shot up, and her emerald green eyes instantly pleaded with me not to. "I just... I need some air."

I needed more than just air, but I didn't want to say that to her.

"I'll come with you," Mom offered quickly. "We can talk and—"

"I think I just need to be alone," I interrupted. My voice was harsh, more so than I expected, but I couldn't bring myself to even apologize. I wasn't mad at all. I was the opposite, actually. I felt terrible that Mom and Grams were so helpless against this force of nature that had buried itself deep inside the strands of my DNA. As much as we fought, and as angry as I'd been with them over the last few days, knowing how many secrets they'd kept from me, I couldn't be upset about this.

It was what it was. That had been made abundantly clear to me. Not only was I a witch, but I was a fae as well.

"Are you sure?" Mom tried again.

"I'm sure." I nodded. "I'll see you tonight, okay? Or in the morning. Don't wait up."

I backpedaled out of the kitchen as fast as my legs could carry me. Miraculously, I didn't run into any of the clutter in my haste to escape this house, the one that suddenly felt like it was closing in around me, suffocating me until all of the oxygen had been drained from my lungs, and then moving into my blood and sucking out the tiny atoms from the bright red liquid, until every single cell in my body was dry and deflated.

I was vaguely aware that my legs took me down the street and out of Portland, into the serene woods about a block away. They were my happy place. They always had been, even when I was too small to understand what unhappiness really was.

I used to think I just liked nature. Who didn't? It felt so good to feel the soil between my toes, to ground myself on the earth.

But now, I had to wonder if there was another, far more mystical reason I loved the woods so much. Maybe because I was part wood nymph, or fairy, or countless other creatures.

None of those answers seemed appealing.

Maybe it would all be fine. After all, what did I *really* know about the fae?

Nothing.

I ducked under the branches of a baby redwood tree and found myself in my favorite clearing. A brook ran through the middle, babbling happily, singing a tune along the backs of the large, flat rocks, one that lifted my soul and brought a sense of calm down over me.

"It's all going to be fine," I whispered to myself. I let my fingertips drift along the top of the cool, smooth water. It felt pure and clean, unmarred by the awful evils of the world around me.

I wish I could say I felt like I was overreacting, but the truth of the matter was that something deep inside me told me that, if anything, I was under-reacting. There were so many reasons I had to be wary of everything I'd found out in, oh, the last two days.

And number one on the list? There were plenty of witches in this town, but no fae. In fact, the only time I'd ever heard Grams mention anything to do with fae was when she was being terribly negative, or downright scary.

Like, for instance, when I was seven and wanted to build fairy houses with my friends. She'd knocked over my poorly built stick and stone hut with a shovel, and then warned me that only people who have bad intentions would ever call a fairy to their house.

So, suffice it to say, I'd grown up thinking fae were bad. I just didn't know they were *real* and bad.

I let out a puff of air and bounced my lips together with the exhale, trying to find some way to calm the anxiety that was just piling up inside my stomach, getting worse by the second. There was no way, of course.

All of a sudden, my phone rang. It went off with that awful, annoying jingling iPhones always do, and just about scared the pee out of me.

Okay, it might have actually scared a tiny bit of pee out of me.

"Jesus," I breathed, scrambling to yank it from my pocket and turn off the annoying song before it could disturb the peace of the forest even further.

To my absolute surprise, Hunter's name popped up on the screen.

And even more surprising? When I saw it there, my stomach did that foolish flipping about it used to do when I first met Kenneth. It was like I had eaten a live spider, and it was scuttling about in there, filled with happiness.

Ugh. I could not fall for Hunter right then. I

couldn't have any sort of feelings for him beyond a nice, professional relationship. One that would end as soon as I knew Mom and Grams were safe.

At least, that's what I tried to convince myself of. All the same, I felt myself smiling when I answered the phone.

"Hey," I said.

"You okay?" The response was immediate. I wasn't even surprised that he knew enough to tell that I felt off in any way. It seemed natural for the two of us, like he should be able to tell from one, singular word that I wasn't in the best of moods.

"Fine," I reassured him, even though it was a lie. "Family stuff, you know?"

There was a long, drawn out pause on the other end of the line. Even over the phone, it felt awkward, stilted. Finally, he cleared his throat, and I could nearly hear him nod on the other end.

"Yeah, totally," he said gruffly. "You just ran out so fast..."

Another pause.

"You didn't call just to listen to me breathe, did you?" I joked.

"Uh, no, of course not," he barked. "We've got another murder. I want you to come down to the scene with me, help me investigate. I've got an in with the police department, and a buddy of mine said he could get us access."

Holy. Crap. On. A. Cracker.

There was nothing better than a fresh crime scene for solving a case. I'd learned that back in Boston, from one of my favorite homicide detectives.

"Text me the address. I'll be right there," I told him quickly. Springing up, I shoved my phone in my pocket and dashed back through the forest to get my Mom's car.

This was it. I could feel it. I was going to solve this case tonight.

14

THANKFULLY, I had the keys to my mom's Mustang in my back pocket, so I didn't have to go inside and tell her where I was going. Call me crazy, but I don't think she would have been totally on board with me going to the crime scene of one of their friend's murders, while putting myself in harm's way.

My heart sank as I realized that they did, in fact, have another dead friend. I wondered who it was, which one of the faces in those ten photos I'd found in the bookshop was no longer in the land of the living?

I really hoped it wasn't the owner of the bookstore. Theodosia. She may have said some weird things to me, and called out my energy, but she had kind eyes.

They all did.

The address Hunter had texted me was actually one I didn't recognize, which was surprising considering I'd grown up here, and prided myself on knowing every nook and cranny of Portland. Though, I suppose that was a hard thing to do when I hadn't lived here in over fifteen years. The modern world had changed the city I knew and loved and twisted it into something unrecognizable.

It was almost funny, in a way, that when I was a barely grown woman, all I'd wanted was to get out of this slow northern town, to venture out on my own and explore the world. I probably would have given my left arm to have Portland the way it was today. But now, I was so far off from that naive little girl, I might as well have been a totally different person.

Even among all of the magic and craziness, Portland was where I belonged. With Mom and Grams, near the sea and under the cloudy, rainy skies. I was supposed to be here. And I probably should have never left.

Maybe I would have discovered my powers earlier, if I'd stayed. Maybe my life would have turned out completely differently. Or, maybe not. I was so hot headed at twenty-one that it was completely possible I would have just cut Mom and Grams out of my life, so angry with the betrayal I ran off to Boston anyhow.

Who knew? I supposed I probably shouldn't dwell too much on the past, though.

The address Hunter had given me, 2374 Acorn Rd., was clear across town and way outside of it, out into the fields and forests of the farmers and hippies. I turned down an old dirt road, surrounded by trees, and shivered when the sun fell away, covered by branches and leaves.

The house was at the very end of the street, all alone, secluded, and set back from the world around it. Admittedly, it was the perfect place for a murder. The killer probably thought no one would find the body for days.

I wondered for a second who had called it in, but my thoughts quickly turned to other, more important things as I put the car in park.

First and foremost was the fact that there was not a single cop in sight. A worried, unsettled feeling landed in my stomach, but I pushed it aside. Maybe Hunter's friend in the department had made sure the scene was cleared for us before Hunter called me down there, so we could have as much freedom to explore the crime scene as possible.

I got out of the car, detritus and tree bark crunching under the old sneakers I'd thrown on that morning, and glanced around. There wasn't a soul in sight. Even the wild animals had disappeared. Whereas the woods around Portland normally teemed with squirrels, rabbits, and even a deer or two, the ones near me were awfully quiet, as if all of the wildlife had run from this place.

As I approached the porch, I could see that the old, rundown red front door was closed tight. One of the little windows had been shattered, which I assumed was how the killer had managed to get inside in the first place.

I grabbed onto one of the old wooden support beams as I stepped onto the porch, and all of a sudden, the world around me melted away as I was transported into a vision.

I hadn't been expecting it, but at least this time, I didn't panic and freak out the way I had when I'd seen Muriel's death. Instead, I was almost fascinated, in a bit of a sick way. I had the ability to see things that most other people didn't. If I wasn't so freaked out about all of the other issues that surrounded me at the moment, I think I could have found it sort of cool, actually.

The room that formed around me looked older, from a different time. I was in a kitchen, behind a long wooden table. The refrigerator wasn't modern at all, but instead looked World War II era.

There was a woman with me. She was beautiful, and young, maybe mid-twenties, with fire engine red hair and bright green eyes that flashed with an excited amazement.

She looked like my Grams.

There was another figure there, too, a horridly evil looking being. I could only see its back, though, as it descended upon the woman like death.

"Well, he wasn't human," it was saying.

The woman conjured up a fireball and laid a hand flat over her stomach.

"Laslow was like me." The creature barked the words, but I could tell he relished them, that each syllable rolling off his tongue was like a good glass of wine at the end of a very long day.

Wait. Laslow. That had been the name Grams had used, the name of my grandfather.

The name of the man who had given me his fae powers.

My eyes popped open. It was my Grams.

The second that realization washed over me,

though, the vision disappeared, replaced with the tattered front porch of the witch's house.

"Oh my God," I breathed.

I wasn't sure exactly what I'd just seen, but it sent me into a twisting spiral of wonder.

Was it possible that Laslow was alive? Could I find him?

The creak of the rickety wooden beams underneath my feet brought me back to earth, and I remembered that I was in the middle of an investigation. My questions could wait until I'd had a chance to get home and see Grams, then tell her all about my vision.

I took another step forward, but a vision flashed before my eyes. It was quick, less than a second. The flash was so fast I almost thought I was imagining things, save for the fact that I knew I didn't have a good enough imagination to conjure up the image I'd just seen.

There was a man, tall and handsome, with well-developed muscles and flowing, white blonde hair. He was dirty, and wore a tattered set of brown pants and no shirt at all. He'd been chained to a mossy stone wall in what looked like a jail cell, and seated underneath a window with uneven, criss-crossing bars over it.

The reason I knew I couldn't have imagined it,

though, was because of what I saw outside that window. A beautiful, majestic mountain, with grass as blue as the sky, and a waterfall that flowed down the center that looked like it was made out of pure fire.

There was no way I could have imagined that image.

"Come back," I murmured to myself, attempting to fall back into the vision. The words were strangled and desperate, but my mind had fled and landed in another world.

I was torn. My emotions were so turbulent that I couldn't pick out one from the other. But I just felt this pull toward what I saw. Was it another world? Hidden within my world? A parallel dimension?

Whatever it was, I knew beyond a shadow of a doubt that I was meant to be a part of it. Some of me was from that world, and I desperately needed to know how to get there.

With even more sureness, though, I knew I needed to get to that cell, and save that man. Because I was pretty darn sure he was my grandfather.

The vision didn't return to me, though, and I was still standing on a porch in the middle of the woods with absolutely nobody around.

I'd been expecting a whole parade of people. That was how our crimes scenes looked back in Boston. But, at the very least, I thought there would be at least one person there.

And Hunter. Where was he? I didn't see a car--not that I even knew what car he drove.

What if the killer had hurt him? Or worse? I knew now that I was dealing with a supernatural murderer.

I felt sick. I launched myself over the next step and dashed across the porch, pushing open the front door with all my might. I may not have known how to use my magic well, or at all, really, but if something was wrong with Hunter, if someone was hurting him, then I needed to try.

I wasn't even sure why, exactly. There were all these feelings swirling around inside me that I didn't like, and sure as heck didn't want to think about. All I could focus on were those wonderful gray eyes and that strange, lopsided smile he gave freely to anyone who needed it. If the witch murderer was on the loose and wanted to get to me, it would be easy to go after Hunter. He was just a human, after all. He had no magical defenses to ward off evil, no way to save himself.

"Hunter!" I called out, my voice bordering on desperate as I entered the run-down cabin.

I turned to my left and saw a kitchen.

Wait. I recognized that kitchen. It was the same one from my vision with Grams. It was about sixty five years older, and far more run-down, and a complete mess, but I knew it was the same one.

This was the cabin she'd been in. This was where she'd confronted that evil, hulking figure when she was...

Well, I didn't know just what she was doing. But she'd clearly been scared.

A thousand thoughts raced through my mind as I tried to figure out what this could mean. Had a witch taken over this cabin and lived here? Was anyone really dead?

Or had this been a way to lure Hunter out here, knowing that I'd come after him.

Frantically, I spun around to a big, empty room that I guessed was meant to be the living room. There was a brick fireplace built into the far wall, but the inside was so full of cobwebs I could tell it hadn't been used in ages. There was nothing else in the room but a thick layer of dust, lit by the dusky sunshine that filtered through the old windows.

I stepped past the threshold of the room, not even looking down to notice the thin white line of salt that trailed from one end of the doorway to the next.

"Hunter?" I called, softly now.

I didn't know why, but that pit in my stomach had widened and grown, until it felt like it was big enough to swallow the entire world in a dark blanket of doom.

15

I GLANCED into all of the corners of the living room, just in case, but it was totally and completely empty. My heart had started to pound, but not in a good way, like when you meet a new friend or go on a date with a guy.

This pounding was a dark, dull thudding that played my ribcage like a drum set, beating off a rhythm that intensified with every passing second.

I needed to get out of there. I'd get in my car and call Hunter from the road. Hopefully he'd answer, and I'd realize I went to the wrong address, or did something else equally foolish.

But if he didn't answer... I didn't know what I would do, actually.

I rushed back toward the doorway, but when I tried to step over the threshold, I was thrown back, violently, by some sort of invisible force. My back slammed against the ground so hard the wind was knocked out of me, and I spluttered and coughed as I tried to regain my breath. The dust was in my hair, my nose, my eyes, my mouth, but I couldn't even focus on that. All I could think about was the fact that I hadn't been able to leave.

Coughing, I forced myself to stand back up, and glared at the doorway.

Then, I tried it again. I strode forward purposefully, planning to trick the doorway into thinking I was completely calm, and then—

BAM!

This time, an explosion of sparks accompanied my rather ungraceful fall to the floor. I saw stars when I slammed to the ground, knocking my head against the hard edge of the bottom of the fireplace.

"What?" I spluttered. I regained my breath and forced myself to my feet a second time. "Is this some sort of magic cage, or something?"

I didn't even know if that was a thing. I realized, for the first time, how wildly out of my depth I was. What the hell had I been thinking, wandering into a supernatural crime scene where all manner of terrible beings could have gotten to me? I was the definition of insanity.

But, insane or not, I still needed to get the hell out of this room.

Squinting, I glanced at the window. I could shatter the panes and climb out that way. I just needed some sort of object, like a loose brick from the fireplace.

"I wouldn't do that, if I were you."

The voice was Hunter's. But, at the same time, it wasn't. It sounded just like him, but it was cold and rough, full of... hate. A deep hate.

I spun around to find that Hunter had appeared in the doorway, and he leaned casually against the frame, just behind a line of pure white salt on the floor.

"Thank God you're here," I sighed, deciding to play dumb for the moment. "I know this sounds absolutely crazy, but I'm stuck in this room. Hunter, someone spelled it so I can't escape. I need you to help me."

I made sure to pump just the right amount of pleading into my tone, hoping beyond hope that there was another explanation for what seemed like a horrible situation.

Actually, horrible was probably an understatement. Because the way I saw it right then, it sort of seemed like Hunter had been the one to trap me in this dusty old room, and that was... awful.

I may not have known him well, but I'd thought he was a good person. Apparently, though, I'd thought wrong.

"I don't think so," Hunter shook his head calmly. "You're going to stay in here until I'm done with you. Until I've done what I need to do."

His words sent a chill of terror down my spine. The pure venom that saturated them was enough to make me want to curl up in a fetal position and sob.

"You're the witch killer," I gasped, completely aghast. How had I not seen it? That was why he'd been so interested in what I thought about the case. It was why he did some strange things sometimes, like grab my hand in strange ways.

It was why he knew so much about magic.

But Hunter's head snapped up, and his gray eyes immediately blazed with an uncontrolled anger.

"Do you really think you're going to confuse me by turning the accusation back on me?" He demanded. "You fae really are all alike, aren't you?"

Oh my God.

How did he know I was fae?

My shock and terror must have shown on my face because Hunter nodded slowly.

"Yeah, I know about that," he replied coldly. "I knew it the moment I touched your hand in the coffee shop on the first day. What, were you looking over the faces you'd killed before, wishing you could do it again?"

"What? Hunter, I—"

"DO NOT PLAY DUMB WITH ME!" His roar was so sudden I stumbled backward, absolutely terrified.

That was when I noticed the dagger by his side, shiny and sharp, ready to kill.

Me.

He wanted to kill me. Because he thought I was the killer.

"Hunter, trust me, you don't know enough about the magical world," I started, pleading with him to understand. "It's not me. I didn't kill any-one. My mom and my grandma are part of the coven being targeted. That's the secret they were keeping from me, the big lie I was so upset about the other day, remember? They hadn't told me I was a witch. They'd lied to me my entire life. And I found out because of these murders. I want to find who did this even more than you, I swear. This isn't just a job to me. This is my family."

For a split second, Hunter's expression softened, and I saw the man I knew underneath his facade. The one who was kind and gentle, if a bit strange. Who had taken me to the park when I was upset and forced me to get some fresh air, and breathe.

That was the Hunter I knew. The one I wanted to be around.

But then, like a mask, his face dropped back into that cold expression.

"You're lying," he accused. "That's what the fae do, they lie. That's why I've been sent here- to take care of our fae problem. I have to kill you, Shannon, before you can hurt anyone else."

I'd already guessed that was what he wanted to do, but hearing the words come out of his mouth made it all the more terrifying. I could feel the panic start to set in, the abject fear of knowing I was trapped in this room with a man who wanted to kill me.

A man who, by the looks of it, wanted revenge for the people he thought I'd murdered.

"Hunter, come on, think about this," I murmured. "Be rational. Why would I be trying to solve this case with you if I was the killer? Why would I ask you about the bag of herbs found in Muriel's mouth? What could I possibly have to gain from giving you clues that would help solve the case if I was really the one who did it?"

Hunter brought the blade out in front of him, and I stumbled back again, just a little bit. Rationally, I knew it did me no good to put space between us when I was trapped in this room. But my body had gone into survival mode, and it was all I could do to keep my heart rate and breathing steady.

"I was sent here to investigate," he murmured, more to himself than to me. "The council said there was a fae here in Portland, targeting and killing witches. You're the only fae I've found."

"But that doesn't mean I'm the only fae here," I interjected.

Hunter's gaze flashed menacingly up to me.

"I'm very good at my job, Shannon," he growled. "I don't make mistakes."

"But you have, this time," I cried. "Please, Hunter, listen to me. I'm fae, okay, you've got that right. But I am not the one you're looking for. My mom and Grams, they're witches. They're *human* witches. I'm mixed... it's a long story, but you gotta believe me."

I was bordering on hysterical as I watched

Hunter play calmly with that knife. I could tell from his demeanor he'd done this many times before.

After all, his name was Hunter. It all made sense now.

"I feel as if I at least owe you an explanation," he finally sighed, scratching a hand through his beard and looking at me sadly. "There was something... between us. I wouldn't feel right about killing you without telling you why first."

"Yes!" I latched onto his words desperately, searching for whatever else I could find. "There is something between us, Hunter. Don't you want to explore that? If you kill me, you will never get that chance. Isn't that something you want to know about?"

I loathed the way I sounded in that moment. Begging did not suit me, and neither did latching onto something as juvenile as a little crush to try and manipulate someone. But if what I had to do to save myself was manipulate Hunter, then I would.

I could see the thoughts flying through his mind as he attempted to wrestle with his mixed bag of emotions. The silence lasted so long I started to hope he might believe me, to understand where I was coming from, and the two of us could go after the real killer together.

Hunter chewed on his bottom lip, and I watched as a tear jiggled at the corner of his eye.

But then, suddenly, he lifted a hand and crooked his finger in the classic motion for "come here."

I was about to snort and tell him that only a crazy person would walk over to a dangerous man wielding a knife when my body started to move of its own accord. I slid across the dirty floor, kicking up dust and debris as I went, pulled by some invisible force I couldn't fight. It was almost like someone had thrown a lasso around my midsection, pinning my arms to my side, and then yanked me to them as fast as they could.

Hunter had magic.

His magical lasso brought me right up against the doorframe, where it then slammed my back against the hard wood. A sob escaped my lips, a tangled mess of fear, pain, betrayal, and absolute terror.

I'd never understood that kind of real, intense terror. The kind that could make a person literally dissolve on the inside.

Until now. I understood it perfectly.

Hunter was right in front of me, towering

over me like a giant, scary Hulk. He held that shiny dagger right up in front of his eyes as he stared down at me.

But what I saw in those steely grays wasn't malice. It was more like… regret mixed with determination.

He didn't want to do this.

"Please," I sobbed out. The sound was so small it was hardly better than a breath, but it hung in the air between us for a long moment, seeming to echo over and over again.

That was the sound of my fear.

"You're a fae," he growled.

It wasn't an accusation, or even a statement. Rather, it seemed like an excuse. This was Hunter's way of justifying something he knew was absolutely wrong, something he'd never be able to take back.

"I'm not who you think I am," I sobbed. "I swear."

Breathing was impossible now. I might just die from oxygen deprivation before Hunter could actually kill me.

Slowly, he brought the dagger forward, right toward my throat.

"I've enchanted this," he murmured. "It's one

of the only weapons that can kill your kind. It... it shouldn't hurt too much."

I think he thought his words would bring me a small semblance of comfort, but all they did was terrify me even more.

"Hunter, the real killer is still out there." My rambling had become desperate, unstable, in my terror. I really thought he could do it.

Hunter was about to kill me. And, as he raised the dagger and brought it even closer to my heart, where he, no doubt, planned to plunge it, I couldn't help myself. I couldn't move a single muscle. Whatever force had brought me to him kept me there, frozen, with no way to defend myself.

So, to hide my tears and try to die with a little bit of dignity, I closed my eyes and waited for the cold, sharp sting of death to strike me right in the heart.

16

THE BACKS of my eyelids were as black as night, and I tried to concentrate on my breathing as I waited, to block out the noise of Hunter's half choked gasps, and what I was sure would be the squelching sound of my flesh and blood when he finally stabbed me.

But that stab never came. I waited, and waited, and finally I thought I might have just missed it, that I'd already died and gone to heaven, or wherever fae go when they're gone.

So, very slowly, I opened my right eye and peeked out at the world.

Hunter was no longer in front of me, but I was still in that dilapidated old cabin. I gasped in both shock and relief, and quickly stumbled backward, back into the semi-safe haven of the living room.

I could move again. That was a good sign.

Quickly, I whipped around until I spotted Hunter against the wall on the other side of the hallway that led into the living room. His hands were on his knees and the dagger was on the floor in front of him as he stared up at me, shaking his head vehemently.

"I couldn't do it." The words were more for him than they were for me. He sounded shocked at himself, shocked that he couldn't complete the task he'd been given by this council of his.

A cold stab of anger shot through my heart as I wondered how many times he'd gone through with something like this before. His entire reaction, all this surprise in his face, made me think that this wasn't the first time he'd been sent to kill someone.

But this sure as hell seemed like the first time he hadn't been able to do it.

"Thank you," I breathed. "Thank you for believing me."

"I don't," he replied quickly, shaking his head hard and fast. "I don't."

It sounded as if he was trying to convince himself more than he wanted to convince me. His expression was hard, but his eyes were soft and full of an uncharacteristic amount of emotion. I could see everything flash through them, all of the worries and wonders, as he tried to figure out just why I was the one he wasn't able to kill.

As much as I liked the fact that I was still very much alive, I kind of had to wonder the same thing.

Why hadn't he been able to kill me?

The silence between us was interrupted when my cell phone rang, blaring that horrible ringtone over and over again. Hunter's head snapped up, and both of us froze. Slowly, he shook his head.

"Do not answer that," he growled. "I don't want you telling any of your fae friends where you are."

I was too scared to disobey him right then. After all, he still held that dagger, and he had all that witchy magic that could pull me to him at any moment.

And God only knew what else he could do.

The ringing stopped, and dead silence fell over us once again.

But then it started up second time.

Hunter tilted his head menacingly, a silent order for me not to retrieve my phone, but I had to. The only people who really ever called me on it were Mom, Grams, and Auntie Deedee, and none of them ever called twice.

This was probably an emergency. A magical killer kind of emergency.

"I have to," I told Hunter.

In a flash, my phone was out of my pocket and I slid my thumb across the screen to answer it.

"Hello?"

"Shannon!" My mother's voice was a frantic, hoarse whisper. "Where are you right now?"

"Uh…" I hedged, trying to figure out how to tell her without alerting Hunter. The last thing I needed was for him to kill them, too, just in case.

Or worse. Kill me and leave my body for them to find.

"I'm out for a walk in the woods," I finally continued, keeping my voice as casual as possible.

"Oh, thank God," Mom murmured. "I need you to stay out there, okay? Whatever you do, do not come home."

My heart started to hammer in my chest at her tone, and fear wrapped its icy fingers around my spine. This was a totally different kind of fear than what I'd felt earlier, though. My own death, I could handle. The terrifying anticipation, the pain, the horror, whatever it was, I knew I could handle it.

But the death of my loved ones? I didn't know a person in the world who could handle that kind of horror.

"Mom, what's going on?" I demanded, my voice rising to high pitched levels that would embarrass even a little girl.

There was no answer for a moment, and I worried that the phone call had been cut off. Or worse.

But then, I heard a crash in the background, loud and heavy, like someone plunking down a giant set of bricks.

"That should keep him out, Elle, but we need a plan." Grams' whisper was hurried and terrified.

"Keep him out?" I screeched. "Keep who out?"

My eyes shot to Hunter, pleading with him to believe me, to help me. I didn't need my mom to answer for me to know who "he" was.

The fae killer had found them. My family was his next target.

"Never mind that," Mom insisted. "I have to go. Shannon, promise me you won't come home."

"No, Mom, I'm coming back!" I cried, shuddering in terror.

"Shannon, you--Oh my God!" My mother's shriek was filled with fear, and sent terror shuddering through me even more intensely. I was crying now, snotty, heavy, panting sobs that wailed out of me like a banshee cry. I was hardly even aware of the sounds that left my body, because my mind was on the killer. Over and over, I just kept seeing that image of Muriel tied to her bed.

Only this time, her young, slim body was replaced with my mom. And then with Grams.

And finally, with me.

"Mom, what's going on?" I demanded. "Talk to me!"

But it was too late. The line went completely dead, and something sinister within told me that my mother hadn't hung up the phone.

"No!" I cried, trying to get the call back. I tapped my mother's phone number frantically, but each time the call started, it ended abruptly, like my cell couldn't get enough service to send the call through.

I looked up at Hunter, who had moved to stand just outside the door of the living room, safely on the other side of the line of pure white salt.

"Please," I begged him. "My family's in trouble. The real killer's still out there, and he's going after my mom and my Grams. They're witches. They're part of the coven. If he kills them, I'll…"

I couldn't even finish the thought. Being without them would be far more than I could possibly bear. The world would cave in around me, burying me in a pile of dirt and ashen rubble, until it eventually crushed me completely. I'd wither away and decay without my family.

Hunter was torn. I could see it in his expression. He wanted to believe me. Deep down, he fought for the good guys. I think. At the very least, it didn't seem like he wanted innocent people to die.

And yet, he still didn't believe me. He'd clearly made up his mind about who, and what, I was before he'd called me here. The mere fact that he hadn't been able to kill me didn't mean that he was on the same side as me.

"There are no sides in this anymore, Hunter," I hissed. "This isn't about what you think of me, no matter how wrong you are. People will die if you waste your time in here, killing me. And not just my family, either. The killer is still out there, on the loose, and you and I both know it will keep going until it gets what it wants. Until it kills thirteen witches."

"I won't let that happen," he growled instantly.

"So you'll let it kill two more in the meantime?" I cried. My feet moved of their own accord, and before I knew it, I was right in front of him again, separated only by the chilly air and the line of salt at our feet. I stared right into his gray eyes, unblinking, praying that he'd find the truth.

"Look at me, Hunter," I murmured. "Do you think I'm lying?"

He opened his mouth to answer on instinct, to give me the response he thought I deserved. But something stopped him when he actually looked into my eyes. He froze, his mouth half open, and tilted his head to look me over.

"I don't know," he finally sighed. "You fae are tricksters, evil, vile beings. I don't know if this is just a game."

"Hunter, I didn't even know I was part fae until I was sitting in your apartment asking you about visions and psychic abilities," I snapped.

I was losing patience with him. I wanted to remain calm, to be soothing, like a hiker is to a wild, unpredictable animal. I didn't want to set him off and make him do something rash.

But my family's lives were on the line. That would make anyone drop all rationality for a while.

Hunter screwed up his face, trying to figure out where he stood on this apparent issue.

God. He was trying to figure out where he

stood on *killing me* and sacrificing my family. I almost couldn't believe I was still standing on my own two feet at that point.

"I'm a hunter," he repeated to himself. "This is what I do. Kill fae. Make sure they can't hurt us anymore."

"Hunter, have you ever actually spoken to a fae?" I asked softly. "Or do you just kill them before they have a chance to persuade you in the other direction?"

It was a fair question. I could already tell that Hunter's belief system had begun to crumble, and I was the catalyst for it. I had thrown off his entire idea of what a fae was, and what a fae was supposed to be.

I just prayed it was enough. Because I was running out of time. More importantly, my family was running out of time.

"No," Hunter growled. "I had to make sure you were really the one. I had to get to know you."

"Because you doubted yourself," I whispered. "Hunter, your doubts were right. I'm not the one. He's still out there, and he's going to kill my family if you don't help me do something about it."

I didn't think he'd believe me. In fact, I was almost certain that those were going to be my last words. But then, like a cloud parting on a rainy, dreary day to finally reveal a few golden rays of sun, something passed over his face, and he nodded.

"Fine," he murmured, his face less than an inch away from mine. "But if I find out you're lying, I swear to God Shannon, I'll make you regret it."

His tone could have frozen lava.

"Okay," I nodded. "Just let me save my family."

And then, finally, Hunter toed the line of salt that kept up the spell to imprison me, and I was free from that living room.

I only had one thing on my mind, though: save my family.

17

HUNTER HAD the knife at my back the entire way out of the cabin. The shiny silver dagger was a cold reminder of his killer instincts, and how very easily he could extinguish the flame of my life, just like that. One hard, smooth jab, and it was all over for me.

I managed to keep the panic at bay, though. The only outward signs I was even a little bit scared were the heavy puffs of breath that escaped my lips every time I exhaled.

"I have to get my keys from my pocket," I told him calmly when we got to the Mustang.

"Slowly," he barked.

I kept my movements small and even, pulling the keys out and opening the door with as much caution as a blind person would. Hunter climbed in first, over the driver's seat and into the passenger side, and then held the knife aloft while I got in.

"Drive," he ordered, pressing the knife into my side, now.

"Okay," I said evenly. "But I'm going to need you to lower that a bit. If we get pulled over because you've got a knife in plain view of the cops, my mom and Grams are as good as dead."

He knew I was right. Even if he used magic or trickery to get us out of a sticky situation with the cops, we didn't have any time at all to spare.

"Fine," he growled. "But if I sense you using any magic, this thing stays at your throat the entire car ride."

"You don't need to worry about that," I informed him. "I don't know the first thing about using my powers."

I sped back down the dirt road at a high velocity. The car bumped along the rocks and gravel in the road, sending us up and down in our seats. I was sure the bottom would be all torn up by the time we were done, but I didn't care. If the worst thing that happened today was a lecture from my mom about ruining her precious Mustang, I'd take it with a smile.

The car trip back home was far too long, even as I completely ignored the speed limit and ran just about every red light in the whole of Portland. Cars honked and pedestrians yelled, but I didn't give a crap.

Hunter did, it seemed. He spent the entirety of the car ride with his non-dagger wielding hand gripping onto the little support bar so hard his knuckles turned completely white.

"Car sick?" I asked jokingly.

"Not in the least," he shook his head, even though he kind of looked like he was about to puke.

About ten minutes after I'd received that frantic phone call from my mother, I pulled up outside our tiny little house. It was backlit by the setting sun, since it was now early evening, and I could see that every single light in the house was off. It looked completely dark and abandoned.

"Oh, no" I breathed, as a newfound sort of terror crawled through my bones. Were they already dead? Was I too late? Had Hunter forced me to waste precious time because he refused to believe me.

I didn't even wait for his say so before I leapt out of the car. If he decided to kill me for it, so be it. He crawled out after me quickly, lowering the dagger just a little bit as he stared at the expression on my face.

I was about to rush into the house, with absolutely no guns blazing because I stupidly had no weapons or way to fight this killer, when Hunter wrapped a hand around my upper bicep and yanked me back.

"What are you doing?" I hissed.

He didn't answer, instead pulling me roughly to crouch down behind the Mustang, out of sight of the house. My heart hammered against my ribs, and I struggled to get free from his grip, but he wouldn't let me go. His eyes were focused on the house and, finally, he had lowered the dagger.

"Shhh," he murmured.

"Hunter, let me go and let me get into that house right this—"

He slapped a rough, warm hand over my mouth and successfully muffled my angry words. I was about to bite his palm, hard, when he shifted his eyes from me to my house, pointing with his chin.

Slowly, I turned my head to see what he was looking at.

Bile filled my throat, and the fear within me sent me into a nearly catatonic state.

There was a figure inside my house, dark and

hulking, wearing those same dark robes I'd seen in my vision of Muriel's death. It was standing in our living room, right in front of the mantle, holding a picture frame.

I bet I knew exactly what picture, too. There was only one on the mantle, a huge one, proudly displayed in a big, silver frame.

A picture of me, Grams, and Mom at my college graduation. All three of us were teary eyed, and Mom's and Grams' faces swelled with pride.

Then, just like that, the creature threw the frame on the ground. I didn't have to hear it to know that the glass had just shattered, spewing shards all across my living room floor.

I glanced back at Hunter, understanding now why he'd pulled me back behind the Mustang.

He saw the light flash into my eyes, nodded, and slowly let his hand come down. Then, to my surprise, he started to lean forward. For a split second, I actually thought he was going to kiss me, and I hated myself a little for the spark of longing that flared up in my stomach.

But our lips didn't meet. Instead, he leaned in until his mouth brushed the outer shell of my ear.

"I believe you now," he murmured quietly, making sure the fae wouldn't be able to hear us.

When he pulled back, I knew I didn't have to

say a thing. All I did was nod, and let my eyes convey my utter gratitude.

I don't know why, but the fact that Hunter believed me suddenly made everything so much better.

I sucked in a quiet breath and turned back toward the house to track the fae's movements.

But the fae was gone. My eyes popped open, and the fear returned.

"We have to find them," I told Hunter. "They're still alive. I know it."

I wasn't completely sure if it was actually knowledge or hope, but I just didn't feel like they were dead. I was sure I would have known, would have felt some sort of cold stab in my heart, or maybe had a vision to tell me the truth.

Hunter studied my face for a moment before he nodded.

"Where would they hide?"

I thought over his question for a moment. I'd never had to prepare for something like this, never had to wonder where we would go if a mad killer somehow made his way into our house.

But Mom and Grams were smart. They'd know that the first thing to do would be to try and get out of that house, if they could.

"The shed in the back," I told him. I was absolutely certain that's where they were. Maybe I just knew them really well, or maybe my psychic fae powers were telling me the truth. Either way, I suddenly knew with absolute certainty that they were in the shed in our backyard, the one that housed all of Grams' gardening tools, and even a few spell books.

Ones that I used to believe were complete and utter crap. If we made it out of this alive, I swore to myself that I'd ask Grams and Mom to teach me everything they knew about magic.

Carefully, Hunter and I crawled out from behind the Mustang and crouched down, walking around the edge of the house and through the tiny gate, into the backyard.

The whole time, I was certain we were going to be attacked at any moment. The fae would leap out at us and slash our throats before we got a chance to move or defend ourselves.

Thankfully, that didn't happen. We padded across the moist grass under the dusk of the evening sun and made it to the shed without being attacked by some sort of monstrous, magical creature.

I didn't even know what fae were, exactly. For all I knew, the thing inside my house could have looked exactly like a Sith Lord from *Star Wars*.

When we got to the yellow shed at the very back of our property, I reached out and tried to open the door, but it was locked.

Of course. Mom and Grams weren't stupid enough to leave it unlocked, even if it would probably do no good against an evil maniac.

"Guys, it's me," I whispered, as quietly as I possibly could. "It's Shannon. Open the door."

Still, silence.

"Some fae can change their voices," Hunter murmured in my ear.

"Okay, uhhhh…" I whispered, searching for some way to prove to them it was really me. "Remember when I was seven, and I decided to run away from home? I packed up a bag and everything and marched all the way down to Auntie Deedee's, and told her that she was my new mom? Would the fae know that?"

Just like I'd hoped, my anecdote did the trick. Quickly, the door swung open, and two pairs of hands twisted up my shirt and then yanked me inside.

Hunter followed quickly, slipping in just before Mom slammed the door shut. She pressed her palms flat against it, bowed her head, and closed her eyes. The door glowed a soft green for a moment, and then the light faded away.

Mom stepped back and stared at me with a soft smile on her face.

"I told you not to come home," she said quietly.

"I was never very good with your rules," I shrugged. "Besides, I brought back up. Meet Hunter."

I gestured toward the man with my arms, and Mom and Grams instantly stared at him.

"Hmmmm, good choice," Grams nodded. "Better than Kenneth. This one doesn't seem so high strung."

"Grams!" I gasped.

How was it possible that even in the middle of a life or death situation, my grandmother still managed to embarrass me like nobody else? There should have been some sort of law against that, as far as I was concerned.

"You're witches?" Hunter asked carefully. It was then that I noticed he still had the dagger wrapped tightly in his grip.

Mom and Grams noticed, too. The two of them sidestepped over to me, Mom putting her hand out to protect me like she had when I was a kid, and glared at him.

"That's a fae killer," Mom said accusingly. "Who are you?"

Hunter glanced down at the dagger, and then back up at me.

"He was sent here to kill the fae," I explained. "He's a..."

It was then that I realized I wasn't exactly sure what Hunter's official title was.

"A hunter," he supplied.

"A hunter named Hunter?' I snickered.

"Yes." He rolled his eyes, and for a moment, everything seemed normal between us.

And then, there was a loud, hard bang against the door to the shed. All of us nearly jumped out of our skin.

The killer knew where we were. And he wanted in.

18

ALL FOUR OF us backed up, standing as far from the door as possible. But that was all we could do. There was no recourse, no way out, as we stood in that tiny little shed surrounded by gardening shears and shovels, and waited with bated breath as the fae tried to get in, ready to destroy us all.

Or, well, destroy Hunter and me. I figured he probably still needed to perform his satanic ritual on Mom and Grams if he wanted to complete his spell. Whatever spell that was.

I grabbed a pair of garden sheers in desperation as a second bang echoed against the door. I knew they'd do no good against a magical creature, but something was better than nothing.

"Well, you're the hunter," Grams snapped at Hunter. "Fight it off."

Hunter nodded, and stepped in front of us with his dagger held high. Even just seeing him put himself in the line of danger twisted my heart.

I didn't want him to get hurt.

BANG!

Another explosion rattled the door to the shed. This one sent dust and spiders tumbling down over us, falling in clouds through the dark space.

Then, a long, low humming started up on the other end of the door.

"It's a woman!" I gasped at the sound. It was too high pitched and far too feminine to ever be a man.

I don't know why that surprised me quite so much. I guess all my time spent as a D.A. in the human world had made me quite averse to the idea of female serial killers.

Then again, this was no regular serial killer.

"*Avare otundum,*" the voice was humming, over and over again.

"What does that mean?" I asked quietly.

Mom's eyes were wide with terror, while

Grams stood behind her, a stern expression on her face.

"Get behind me, Shannon," Mom ordered.

But before I could do anything else, the humming stopped, and all of a sudden the door exploded off its hinges in a blast of orange light and wood shards.

And then we were face to face with the demonic fae.

Only, she didn't look evil, on first glance. In fact, she looked almost normal. She was tall, maybe five eleven, and thin, with long brown hair that fell past her waist and piercing brown eyes with hints of evil in them. Her figure was obscured by her giant black robes that swathed her entirely, like a wizard from the Middle Ages. Her skin was perfect, ageless, and nearly translucent. It actually seemed to glow a soft, pearly white, almost like a ghost.

Slowly, the woman appraised the four of us, a smile on her face.

"Witches," she intoned, pointing at Mom and Grams. "Good. Two more for my ritual." Then, her malevolent eyes traveled over to Hunter. She raised a brow and licked her lips in appreciation. "I didn't know hunters could look like you."

Finally, her gaze traveled over to me. Her cold

eyes narrowed, and I saw confusion flash in them. She quickly stuffed it away, though, not willing to show any signs of weakness in front of her prey.

"And you," she murmured quietly. She pressed her lips into a thin line, trying to figure out just what I was. "You are not a natural being, my dear. What are you?"

"None of your business," I snapped.

A high, cold laugh filled the air, and she raised a brow.

"Spunky," she chuckled.

All of a sudden, I was flying across the floor toward her, just like I had flown toward Hunter in the cabin, completely against my will. I was vaguely aware that Mom screamed, and Hunter cried "No!"

But mostly, I was focused on this woman. Fae. Person. I didn't even know what to call her. Honestly, if I'd met her on the street, I might have wanted to be her friend.

I kept my fear in check as I came face to face with her. We were uncomfortably close, and not just because she was an evil killer.

Her hand flew up, and there was a crunching sound behind me, followed by Hunter's pained cry. I whipped my head around and was barely able to see Hunter crumpled on the ground, holding his arm as if it was broken. Mom crouched over him, trying to help.

But then, a pair of icy cold fingers latched under my chin and forced my head to turn back toward the fae.

"You are powerful, my child," she murmured. "What are you doing with these fools? You could be so much more. You are so much more."

"Don't talk about them like that," I snapped. "You don't know the first thing about me."

I grabbed her hand and shoved it roughly away from me, but that didn't faze her one bit.

"Yet," she responded evenly.

That single word held so much pride and power in it. But it also held a gross overstatement of how persuasive she thought she was. I didn't know who this woman was, or why she thought I belonged with her, but I didn't care.

Suddenly, there was a firestorm of anger inside of me. It flared up like a sudden earthquake, bringing with it more emotion than I'd ever felt in my life, all at once. The thought of this woman trying to, what, team up with me? Well, whatever it was she thought we were going to do, I was not having it.

And apparently, neither was my magic.

All of a sudden, there was a blinding flash of

pure white light that surrounded the woman and me. A loud, electric shriek accompanied it, and then, a second later, the two of us were in the middle of the backyard, far away from the shed.

"Shannon!" Hunter's cry was strangled by pain, but I couldn't even spare a glance back at him.

The woman was on the ground in front of me, but she stood calmly, brushing dirt off her robes, and appraised me with an almost proud expression.

"How fascinating," she murmured. "You didn't even have to say a spell."

"Yeah," I barked. All I was really trying to do, though, was hide the fact that I had no freaking clue how I'd just done... whatever I'd just done. All I knew was that I'd gotten angry, and then the next second we were in the middle of the yard.

I'd just wanted to get her away from my family.

"*Lumanesca!*" The woman yelled, throwing her hand up above her head.

A bolt of orange light shot out of her hand, webbing out like a spider, and surrounded us in a net of bright, hot light. I could feel the power rolling off of it in waves, and instinctually knew not to get any closer to it. I wasn't sure exactly what would happen, but I sure as hell didn't want to find out.

Hunter seemed to know, though. He bolted out from the shed, dagger in hand, and sprinted toward me.

"Don't do this to her!" He yelled at the fae.

But it was no use. He slammed up against the bright orange net and was thrown back, shivering from what I could only guess was electrocution.

"Don't hurt him!" I screamed, the sound tearing from my throat in a wail of terror.

"Don't worry, I'm not interested in them anymore." The woman laughed. It was a high, cold sound that shook me to my very core and split my eardrums in two. "No, now I am very much interested in you, darling girl. Who are you? Where did you come from?"

"I'm not answering any of your questions," I spat.

I needed to get out of this. I needed her vulnerable so Hunter could use his special dagger to kill her. My brain didn't know what to do but somehow, my body did.

Those intense waves of emotion thundered through me, and a bolt of bright white light shot from my hand. I lifted it instinctively, directing the bolt straight toward the fae murderess. It smacked her square in the chest, but she managed to stand her ground.

The orange net, however, didn't fare quite as well. Out of the corner of my eye, I caught it flickering, blinking in and out of existence as the fae regained her balance.

When she started to stand, though, it began to come back into focus.

A smile spread across my face. I took a breath, and summoned all of that emotion, willing this bright bolt of energy to return to my body.

It did.

Bolts shot out of either one of my hands, smacking the woman in the chest in quick succession. And then they kept coming, one after the other, knocking her backward. And with each stumbling step she took, each stilted breath, the orange net of energy flickered around us and started to dissolve.

Finally, it was gone completely, and the fae woman was nearly flat out on the ground, breathing heavily and glaring up at me with evil eyes.

But at that point, I was bone tired. Every bit of adrenaline-fueled energy I'd had before flew from me, leaking out along with the white energy.

Gasping, I hit my knees, hunched over on the ground as I did everything I could to remain conscious.

"Shannon!" Mom gasped, running up to me. I saw her coming out of the corner of my eyes, but so did the fae.

"*Fiemortem!*" She screeched.

I didn't need to know spells to translate what that meant. Her body language alone was enough to tell me what spell she was attempting to cast.

"No!" I hollered.

A blue orb of energy zipped from the fae's outstretched hand, headed straight toward mom's chest. For a moment, it was as if time froze. Mom's green eyes were wide, and she was mid-stride, trying to duck the killing spell.

The fae was on the ground, a wicked smirk on her face. But her eyes weren't focused on my mom. She was looking straight at me.

I didn't think. My body just moved on instinct. All I knew was that if I didn't act, my mom was about to die.

So, without another thought, I mustered up the last, tiny bit of my energy, leapt to my feet, and dove right in front of that blue ball, absorbing all of the energy into my own body before it could hit my mom.

Just like that, time sped up again. I slammed to the ground, hard. The world exploded around me in bright flashes of blue, white, and orange light. Dirt flew, grass sailed, and people screamed.

I think I may have been one of them.

An immense pain overtook my entire body, twisting and burning through the whole of my being, seeming to invade even the nuclei of my atoms as it ripped through me, burning hot and bright. I'd never known pain like that before.

The world became a blur. Explosions, screams, pain.

There was nothing else.

I don't know how long I held on for, how long I clung desperately to life. I couldn't move, or do anything at all, really. But I knew I couldn't die. If I did, there would be no one standing between the people I loved and a murderer.

But eventually, no matter how hard I tried, that blue ball of dead overtook me.

The last thing I remember seeing was my Mom's terrified face as she knelt next to me, sobbing and murmuring countless spells, trying to save my life.

I don't think it worked.

19

THE NEXT THING I KNEW, I was on a cloud. At least, that's what it felt like. My eyes were closed, and I just felt comforted, like I didn't have a worry or care in the world.

I couldn't remember where I was, or exactly what had just happened. But I knew whatever I was laying on was soft and cool, and smelled of lavender, just like my Grams. The scent wrapped me in a blanket of comfort. My entire body was warm, and I felt the strongest sense of calm I'd ever felt in my life.

I wasn't fighting an evil fae. I wasn't begging Hunter to spare my life. I wasn't jumping in front of a blue ball of death.

I just existed. And it was so peaceful.

Slowly, my eyes blinked open, seemingly of their own accord. At first, the world was bright and out of focus. All I could see was bright golden sunlight. It came down on me, heaven-like, and surrounded me in a pool of yellow warmth.

Slowly, the rest of my world started to come back into focus, and I realized I recognized my surroundings.

I was in my mom's room. There was her dresser across from me, with the giant mirror on top of it. A pile of clothes was on the floor next to the bed. Knowing Mom, they were probably perfectly clean outfits that she'd discarded that morning, deeming them unfit for wearing that day.

Then there were the smells--lavender, sage, and incense, along with the soft floral of her favorite perfume.

It must have been heaven. Everything around me had been perfectly chosen to bring me comfort while I slipped into the afterlife. Honestly, I found myself thinking that it wasn't all that bad. If I could live in my mother's bedroom forever, surrounded by the sights and scents that brought me the most comfort, I thought I'd be pretty okay.

"Shannon."

Even her voice was still with me, soft and comforting.

"Shannon," she repeated. A soft, warm hand stroked my cheek a few times, and I blinked again.

Once more, the room settled into focus, but the hazy white glow had disappeared. It all felt far too real to be heaven.

Slowly, I turned my head, and found my mother's worried, but smiling, face above me. Her long red curls tickled my nose, making me want to sneeze.

I batted them away with my hand, and then wiggled the rest of my body.

I felt very much alive.

"Thank God you're awake," Mom gasped. A wail settled in her throat, but she quickly shut it down. Instead, she crawled up into the bed next to me and wrapped me in her arms. "I thought I was going to lose you."

"No way," I chuckled. "You're stuck with me for another forty years, lady."

"I wouldn't have it any other way," she sighed. Quickly, though, my mom pulled back and stared at me sternly. "What were you thinking? That spell could have killed you! It should have killed you."

"But it didn't," I pointed out. "And it definitely would have killed you. Then the fae- oh my God, the fae!"

I sprang bolt upright, accidentally clunking Mom's chin on the way up, and looked about in terror.

"Ow!" She cried indignantly.

"Where is she? What happened? Is she dead?" I demanded, the questions spewing from my mouth like a geyser.

Mom sucked in a deep breath, bit her lip, and shook her head.

"I don't think she's dead, Shan," she sighed. "But something happened when you absorbed her spell. Something... I don't know how to explain it. It was almost like you turned into this big ball of energy yourself, and then all of a sudden you were back, passed out on the ground, and the fae was gone. I don't know where she went."

"Damn." I shoved my face in my hands, trying not to let the terror overtake me again. The woman's face floated behind my black eyelids, almost like it was taunting me.

Somehow, I knew this wasn't over. She'd be

back to finish what she started, to kill an entire coven of witches.

With a start, I remembered the way she'd spoken to me.

"Mom," I murmured, trying to push myself up higher on the bed.

"Don't sit up," she ordered, shoving my shoulders back down. "what do you need? Coffee? Pop Tarts?"

"No," I shook my head. "Mom, the fae's going to be back. She seemed very interested in me."

Mom sighed and nodded her head.

"I figured," she murmured. "I think anyone would be interested in you, baby. You may not have a deep understanding of our world just yet, but there is no one like you out there. There's gonna be a hell of a lot of people who want to get in on what you are."

The tone of her voice made my stomach twist up in knots. My mom would never lie to me, but I also knew she'd never tell me something as serious as that unless she thought it was absolutely necessary for my survival.

"Wait, where's Hunter?" I gasped, suddenly realizing I didn't know what had happened to him.

Mom gritted her teeth together and rubbed a hand across her forehead.

"Your friend disappeared right after the fae did," she replied. "I'm afraid your Grams and I were a little bit too wrapped up in making sure you didn't die to keep an eye on him."

"Mom, no, we need to find him," I replied.

There was a twofold reason I wanted Hunter back in front of me. One was, well, I was fairly sure I had a tiny little crush on him.

But the second was far more important. I needed to make sure Hunter didn't plan on flapping his lips about my secret identity as a half-fae, half-witch to anyone on that council of his. Call me crazy, but I didn't think they'd take too kindly to my existence.

In fact, I was pretty sure they'd make an effort to squash out my existence the first chance they got.

"Shannon, look, I know you," she sighed. "I know there was something about this man that you liked, and I get it, really. Trust me, do I get it. The number of men over the years that I have fallen for—"

"Mom, that's not what—"

"Let me instill some motherly advice here, okay?" She interrupted. "Hunters are not good people. They're not witches or warlocks, even.

They're humans that the witch council deemed cruel and relentless enough to turn into fae hunting monsters. Their magic was given to them. They weren't born with it. They don't have the same ideals of right and wrong as we do, the same notion of who's good and who's bad. If you get in their way when they're going for the kill, they won't hesitate to kill you, too."

Her words were cold and angry. I thought about Hunter's face back in the cabin when he'd been trying to shove that dagger through my heart.

That didn't seem cold and vile to me. He seemed so human in that moment. I couldn't imagine that he was this same type of horrid man Mom described.

But it didn't matter. Because I didn't want him for the reasons she thought I did.

"Mom, that's not what this is," I said quickly. "I don't like him... okay, look, this isn't about my feelings for Hunter. He knows what I am. He thought I was the one killing witches. That's why he was with me. He trapped me in this cabin out in the woods, and he tried to kill me. But he couldn't."

Mom's brows knitted together in utter confusion. She blinked twice, and then adjusted the blanket underneath her over and over again as she tried to make sense of my words.

"He didn't want to kill you?" She murmured. "Are you absolutely sure?"

"Yes," I replied. "And I think that the witch council might be after him now. He failed them, after all."

"The council is unrelenting," Mom sighed.

Suddenly, the door burst open, and Grams strode in carrying a tray full of fried, greasy food. There were popovers, chicken and waffles, biscuits with country gravy, and a big mug of coffee.

"I thought I heard voices in here," she announced, plopping the tray down on the dresser. She came over to stand behind Mom and brushed a piece of my hair back from my face. "How ya doing, child?"

"Okay," I replied. But Grams just raised an eyebrow, knowing full well I was lying. "I'll live. Isn't that what's important?"

"Well, seeing as you gave us quite the scare back there, I'd say it's pretty darn important," she chuckled. "Now, are you hungry?"

What is it with grandmothers and food? Why do they always bring it whenever someone's feeling sick? It's like their magic cure all.

I glanced over at the tray of heavy food. As appetizing as it looked, the thought of putting anything in my mouth at that moment seemed like the worst possible idea in the entire world.

"Maybe later," I told her.

"Okay," she shrugged. "But I'm holding you to that, got it?"

"Got it," I laughed.

Silence fell across the room, and Mom and Grams just stared down at me, their eyes full of tears they refused to shed in front of me.

"Well, Elle, I suppose we should get out of here and let the girl have some rest," Grams said.

"Yes," Mom replied. She bent over and kissed my forehead softly, then straightened up, staring at me the way she had when I was a child. "Don't get out of this bed until you've gotten at least five more hours of sleep."

"Yes ma'am," I laughed, rolling my eyes.

But the truth was, it made me feel safe to know I was loved like that.

Mom and Grams turned and were almost out the door by the time I remembered that I had something I desperately wanted to ask them.

"Hey, guys, wait," I called out. They turned back around curiously. "I was wondering...

Grams, do you know what actually happened to Laslow?"

Grams shook her head slowly, pain soaring across her face.

"No," she sighed. "I wish I did, baby. I wish I could give you some answers."

I could tell by the look in her eyes that she really wanted them. For a moment, I wrestled with whether or not I should mention my vision. I didn't want to bring any more hardship upon them, or dredge up more past, painful memories. Especially for Grams.

But that image of the man in the cell, chained to the wall like an animal, flashed through my head again.

If that really was him, if he'd been locked away like that for nearly sixty-five years, I couldn't stay silent.

Grams needed to know. He'd been her one true love, and she deserved some answers.

"I think I had a vision about him," I said carefully, recalling the way they'd reacted to my last one. "I think I saw him. Grams... I think Laslow's still alive."

Grams mouth popped open, and a waterfall's worth of tears filled her eyes.

"Are you sure?" She murmured. "Alive... I

don't... why didn't he find me? Why didn't he come back?"

"He couldn't," I told her quickly. "I'm not totally sure what I saw, but he's someone's prisoner. He was chained up to a wall. And... Grams, I think he was in another world."

20

Hunter

I KNEW Shannon would be fine. When I saw her jump in front of the fae's spell to save her mother, my heart stopped for a moment, but then I remembered the power I'd felt flowing through her that day in the coffee shop.

She'd be fine.

Everything had happened so fast in that moment. The fae had been shocked and aghast, angry that Shannon had ruined her perfect plan. But all the power that exploded out of Shannon must have scared the fae, because I blinked, and then she was gone.

I'd watched as Shannon's mom and grand-mother had rushed over to her, terrified, and completely forgot I was there.

Which was good. That was how it needed to be. They should forget about me, just as I should forget about Shannon.

I was a hunter. I was meant to kill the fae, and anything else that threatened the balance of the world, that tried to send it into a place of evil. And Shannon was fae.

But really, Shannon was unknown. And the hunters didn't like the unknown. We'd rather kick it out of existence than risk letting it live and turning into something worse.

I knew what would happen if I stayed. My in-stincts would take over, and I'd try to kill Shannon again. Her mom and grandmother would stand in my way, and I'd kill them, too. It would be a horrible, messy bloodbath.

Because if I stayed, I knew it would come down to her or me. If I didn't kill her, the council would have me killed.

So, while everyone was distracted with Shannon laying there on the ground, I dashed around the back of her shed and into the woods behind her house.

And then I just kept on running. I cradled the hand the fae demon had broken. Shannon's mom had tried to heal it, to help me, but she'd gotten distracted before she could finish the job. It hurt like hell, but I'd make it through.

I had to get out of there. I wasn't sure where I'd go, exactly, but I knew I had to be far away from Shannon. Let some other hunter get put on her case and forced to try and kill her. If I was right about how powerful she was, she'd kill them first, anyways.

But it couldn't be me. I couldn't be the one sent to kill her. Because I was starting to think I might have feelings for this strange, unnatural woman.

So I ran through the woods, sticks and leaves crunching under the thick soles of my boots. I just kept on running.

Until suddenly, my feet froze, as if they were held in place by some invisible force.

"Shit," I murmured. I knew exactly what was about to happen. It was the same thing that had happened the first time I'd met the council, back when they'd turned me from a regular human into a fae-murdering machine.

Just as I suspected, I started to get sucked

away from the woods. It felt as if my body had been lifted into a vacuum. I was being compressed and stretched all at once as I flew through the atoms of the universe, over fields and house and cities until finally I landed on a cold stone floor. The ground was slimy with moisture underneath my hands, and I struggled to regain my breath.

I knew exactly where I was. It was someplace I hoped I'd never have to be again.

"Hunter," a voice boomed from above me. "Stand."

Slowly, I got to my feet, wiping my hands off on my pants, and looked up at the circle of massive stone chairs above me.

I was in the dark caves of the Hunter's Council. Even after all this time, I'd never been able to figure out just where those caves were. They could have been anywhere on earth. Or even not on earth, for all I knew.

I glanced at the hooded faces above me. Eleven chairs. Eleven masked figures. Three women and eight men. I'd counted the last time I was here, using the voices to try and figure out who was who.

The leader was a man with a deep, booming

voice. His chair was always at the head of the circle, right where the twelve would have been if they were a clock.

I'd never seen their faces or heard their names. I'd never even seen another hunter here. All I knew was that they were more powerful than I could ever hope to be. They'd even given me my magic, which meant that they controlled it.

"Council," I said, kneeling on the stone floor to show my respect.

Silence hung in the air. Then, a woman to my right spoke. Her voice was high and nasally, and she was angry.

"You failed, hunter," she snapped. "You have never failed before. What happened? The Council demands to know."

"The fae was too powerful, ma'am," I told her. "I couldn't fight her. I'm not sure who she was, but I need backup, help. I'm afraid she's going to keep going after witches. She has done it before, after all."

"We are no longer interested in this fae killer," the leader boomed. "It would appear she has a new target, and so do you."

That was when my heart froze in my chest.

I just knew they were talking about Shannon. I wasn't even sure how they knew about her, or how much they knew, but I knew enough about this world to know that they'd see Shannon as a threat. It didn't matter what the truth was. She was different, and insanely powerful, and in this world, different and powerful was not a good thing.

"I don't know what you mean." I was trying to play dumb, hoping beyond hope that there was something else out there they needed me to do.

Another man laughed, a deep roar from his belly. It sounded to me like an old-fashioned king laughing when he made his poor jester dance and make a fool of himself.

The laugh of a coldhearted man.

"Do not play dumb with us, hunter," he demanded. "Or do you forget we hold your life in our hands?"

To prove his point, the councilman shot his arm out and muttered something incoherently.

Suddenly, I was brought to my knees by an invisible force, made to prostrate myself in front of the council, while the dagger in my pocket shot out and hung above me, ready to slit my throat on the councilman's smallest command.

I held my fear in, though. I refused to give them the satisfaction of knowing that they scared me.

Chuckles of mirth skittered about the room as members of the Hunter's Council watched this man hold my life in his hands.

Then, the force lifted, and the dagger clattered to the ground. I let out the breath I hadn't even realized I'd been holding, and forced myself back to my knees, glaring at the man.

"How could I forget?" I spat. "You would never let me."

"That is right," he replied evenly.

"Enough!" Barked the leader. "Hunter. You know very well I speak of the half breed. She is a danger to us all."

"Shannon could never be a danger," I shouted. "She's good, and kind. She can't help what she was born as."

"I do not care about what is in her heart," he snapped. "I care about the power that rolls through her body. It is too much power for any one person to have, witch or fae. We must do away with her."

That was it. Those were the words I knew were coming.

"No," I shook my head. "Please don't make me do this."

"Hunter, I hereby order you to dispose of the half breed, by power of this council," he boomed. "You will do it, or you will die."

A loud, thunderous boom filled the air, like the clap of lightning against water. Then I was sucked right back into that horrible vacuum before I could even think to protest.

When the world fell back into place around me, I realized I was in Shannon's backyard.

My heart sank into my feet.

I glanced up at the house, where I had a perfect view through her bedroom window. Ducking behind a tree, I waited to see if I could catch a glance of her through the double-paned glass.

But she couldn't see me. I was afraid that, if she did, she'd come down here to see me, and then I'd have no choice. We'd be alone, and I'd already learned her weaknesses.

I'd know exactly what to do. The hunter inside of me would take over, and Shannon would be dead.

My breath hitched at the thought. I wasn't sure what my feelings about her were, exactly, but I knew she'd stirred something within me. A humanity of sorts, one that I'd buried long ago, well before I'd even become a hunter.

Just as I'd hoped, Shannon appeared in front of the window to gaze out across her backyard.

Her red hair was frizzy, and there were bags under her eyes as she stared down at the spot where she'd fought the fae the night before.

The ground was singed, a reminder of the great power she held within her. The blackened grass still sparked every once in a while with strange white embers, as if even the ground itself could feel her magic.

I glanced back up at Shannon to find her wiping tears from her eyes. In that moment, all I wanted to do was hug her, to wrap her up in my arms and tell her that everything was going to be alright. She could get through this. She was stronger than any woman I'd ever met.

I couldn't do any of that, though. If I even so much as stepped near her, I'd be overtaken by the intense need to kill. I'd fought it off last time, had been unable to actually ram my dagger through her heart.

But this time, I wasn't so sure I'd make it. Especially now that it was a choice between her life or mine.

As much as I hated to admit it, at the end of

the day, I was a survivalist. When it came down to it, I knew I'd pick me. I had to.

I always had to.

Which was why I needed to put as much distance between Shannon and me as was possible.

I glanced up at her again, but this time, I found that her emerald green eyes had landed squarely on me. She watched me from her bedroom window, her expression stern.

There was fear in her eyes. Fear of me.

Good.

I needed it that way. The more I terrified her, the more likely she was to stay away from me.

Shannon cocked her head, conveying with her eyes what she couldn't say out loud. I knew exactly what she was trying to tell me.

She wanted to talk. She wanted me to come up to her bedroom so we could have some sort of heartfelt moment, where we realized we had feelings for each other and promised to explore them, despite all the craziness in the world around us.

But that was a movie moment. That didn't happen in real life.

Shannon stepped forward, pleading with her eyes, begging me to talk to her.

"We need to work this out," her eyes said. "I want to work this out."

But I shook my head.

"We can't."

I wanted to tell her that the council had put a hit out on her, that her life was in danger.

But then I reminded myself that I could draw this out. For now, her life was only in danger if I was anywhere near her.

Emotion swelled in my chest as I watched this beautiful woman standing at her window.

But then I saw the decision cross her face, the moment where she decided it didn't matter that I was standing here shaking my head. Shannon wanted what Shannon wanted, and she was going to get it.

So, as she turned away from the window, fully intent on coming down to meet me, I slowly backed into the woods behind her house.

I saw when she came out the back door to search for me, heard the emotional sigh she let out when I wasn't there.

"Hunter?" She called out, peering into the woods, where I was safely hidden in the shadows.

But even as she came forward to investigate, I backed further away, until finally, I was up in a tree and watching while she searched the forest floor.

And when she gave up and went back inside, I fled like a bat out of hell. For now, I had only one goal.

Put as much distance between Shannon and I, before I was compelled to kill her.

Start Reading Book Two Now!

READ BOOK TWO!

Divorce, Divination and. . . Destiny?
(Midlife Mayhem Book Two)

WANT A FREE BOOK?

Join Melinda's Newsletter and Claim Your
Freebie!
Potions and Pearls
Join at: https://melindachasebooks.com/

ALSO BY MELINDA CHASE

Midlife Mayhem Series

1. *Forty, Fabulous and . . . Fae?*

2. *Divorce, Divination and . . . Destiny?*

3. *Spandex, Spells and . . . Shadows?*

4. *Paranoia, Pixies and . . . Prophecies?*

5. *Heels, Hexes and . . . Heirlooms?*

6. *Truths, Tricks and . . . Traitors?*

7. *TBA*

8. *TBA*

Accidentally Magical at Midlife?

1. *Gone with The Witches*

2. *TBA - Coming March 2021*

3. *TBA- Coming April 2021*

4. *TBA Coming May 2021*

5. *TBA - Coming June 2021*

6. *TBA*

I

FREE PREVIEW - GONE WITH THE WITCHES

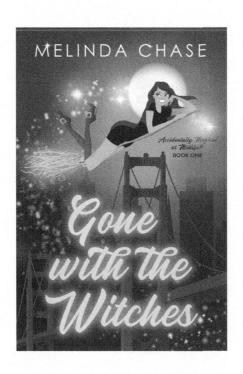

1

CALLIE

MY TOES CURLED open and closed, rubbing my feet against the bright blue, long threaded rug beside my bed.

No, it didn't match the more romantic and subtle look of my room, but Willa bought it for me, wanting to force me to "add some brightness" to my life. Truth be told, Willa was about as much brightness as one person could take at any given moment.

As my best friend, and as gun shy as I could be at times letting people in, she never had to go through the droning process of my inner workings, picking her apart even though there was nothing wrong with her. She was the perfect level of friend, right from the get-go. In fact, for years, at that point, I hadn't really made any other friends. Unless you counted the handful of regulars that frequented the *Lustrous Bean*, a quirky little bookstore and coffee shop that Willa and I had opened back when it was socially acceptable for me to be single, weird, and aloof. Unfortunately, forty years old wasn't as kind when it came to narrow eyed stares in Willa's direction, or mine.

But fuck it, who cared? I was doing my thing the best way I knew how, and so was Willa. That's about as much as I could expect from myself at that point in life. I was content, happy even... most days. Having our shop situated in the small seaside town of El Granada didn't hurt. Every day, I'd walk outside, experiencing the gorgeous views of the ocean, and our shop got the gorgeous views of the copious amounts of tourists venturing out from Half Moon Bay. For me, it was the perfect location.

My phone buzzed loudly on the bedside table and I threw my wild red hair back, pulling the knotted mess out of my eyes. Glancing over, as if I didn't already know who was calling, I was suddenly thankful to the feverish workers in some smog covered city across the ocean for creating the vibrating feature on my phone. Otherwise, I would have been half awake, trying to fumble through the millions of buttons in an attempt to switch off the ringtone Willa had attached to her contact. It was some way-too-poppy, hip for only the 12-year-olds, boy band. I couldn't handle boy or band at those ridiculous morning hours.

"I'm awake," I sputtered into the phone, forcing my eyelids as wide as they could go. "I'm here. I'm awake."

Willa chuckled...or giggled, as she always did, on the other end. "I figured. Just wanted to double check 'cause you owe me a chocolate filled croissant and one of those fancy coffees that we don't make here."

Yawning, I stretched my arms up over my head and nodded at my wild reflection in the mirror hanging over the adjacent dresser. "Right. Right. But don't you think it might turn off customers if we're standing by the coffee machine drinking coffee from a different shop?"

"I thought you might say that." She was far too chirpy for that hour. "I pulled out the box of coffee cups we had bought to sell in the shop, but never got around to putting in a display. I'll just pour it in one of those."

My face curled as I stood, cracking my sore back. Eight years on my feet daily and I still felt like I had run a marathon the day before. It was probably the chocolate filled croissants. "At least we'll get some sort of use out of them. Most expensive excuse to buy someone else's coffee ever."

Willa chirped on the other end. "Well, take a shower, and get your behind in here. All the baking is done, not that we bake more than a rack of cookies, and the coffee is brewed and ready for our morning patrons."

"Mhmm," I said, yawning again as my feet dragged along the wood floors toward the inevitable Arctic chill of my bathroom tile. "I'll be there soon. Just gonna wake myself up and get presentable."

"Don't forget to feed your kids," Willa said, laughing, before hanging up.

I dropped the phone on the dresser as I passed, glancing over at my Basset Hound, Bean, who was still laid out across the end of the bed. He was nothing like most dogs, ignoring his full bladder to catch a few more moments of sleep before I let in Mr. Hobbles, my three-legged cat. They were the kind of friends that shouldn't be around each other more than a few hours a day. They lived to annoy the hell out of each other. But, despite Mr. Hobbles' missing leg, from birth, he was quite nimble, bouncing up and down on Bean every morning when I opened up the bedroom door.

I was just glad they couldn't talk. I couldn't even imagine the never-ending treasure trove of animalistic threats that would constantly haunt my home life. At least I had them to greet me when I came home. They were weird like me. I appreciated that.

Per my usual morning routine, I took about five minutes to stand in the scolding hot water, my face clenched, letting the prickling of my skin subside as my body got used to it. It woke me up pretty quickly. I used the bath soaps I got from the small boutique down from the shop, loving the way my entire bathroom became the entry way to an overly-perfumed, mall-located corporate bath store. I could have stood there for hours, but alas, Willa called from the jungle of books and brews, wanting her morning croissant and "fancy coffee."

After about ten minutes of pep talking myself, and the sound of Bean finally regretting the entire bowl of water he had drank before bed, I pried myself from the sauna-like shower stall and opened the door back to my room. The steam rolled out into the room as I emerged, ringing the water from my hair. Bean whimpered, plopping down next to the bedroom door, his ears swinging, waiting for me to open it and release him to the wilderness of my twenty-foot-square fenced backyard. From the looks of the paw swiping beneath the door, Mr. Hobbles had woken as well, primed and ready for the games to begin.

"Okay, let me get dressed," I huffed, as if either of them had actually offended me.

I pulled out my normal gear, the clothing of champions, a true testament to my entrepreneurial success... black yoga pants and my *Lustrous Bean* t-shirt. Of course, there was absolutely no yoga in my life, except for the few times I tilted my head at the women in the online ads and wondered if a dash of flexibility would be good for me. That motivated spirit lasted until I sat down to another cup of coffee and a new book. No, I dressed for comfort, and of course, to show off the merchandise that we had in piles of boxes in the storeroom, waiting for the unsuspecting tourist to snatch up three for the kids, and one for Aunt June who couldn't make the trip.

I was a walking billboard.

As I moved through the house, I checked each morning routine item from my list, let Bean do his roundabout sniff and piss in the backyard, fed them both, and blew them one wide kiss before heading out for the day. My flip flops slapped against my heels as I made my way to the car, waving at Chuck, the insurance guy, across the street, looking like he was loathing his entire existence as he nodded back and threw his briefcase in the back seat. He handled the thing like the post office handled fragile packages. Whatever was inside was doomed, which was probably nothing. I had a theory that briefcases were never actually used to carry important documents. They were status symbols, good gifts for dads on father's days, and thank you gifts from companies for giving twenty years of your life to indentured servitude.

Maybe that was what I'd get myself when we hit our ten-year mark at the shop, a nice faux leather briefcase with my name etched in the top. I'd carry chocolate croissants and flyers for the *Lustrous Bean* everywhere I went. I would be like the middle aged, weird Santa of El Granada. Chocolate would ooze from my briefcase but that was fine, because Willa was obsessed with the damn things. She'd take care of the mess.

As I drove past Willa's house, just five houses down from mine, I chuckled at her gnome collection. They were all situated in her front flower bed, facing one another as if they were speaking to each other. She always said it made her feel like home, which was odd considering I hadn't really noticed gnomes parading around through California anytime recently. Then again, I didn't really know that much about Willa's past really. She could have grown up in the circus for all I knew. But in the end, our past didn't define us, or at least that was what I attempted to tell myself twice a month at my therapist's office.

I wasn't even sure why I still went. Willa was enough of a therapist, and I didn't have to pay her in any currency except chocolate croissants.

When I pulled into the space in front of the competition, I was happy to see that they weren't yet filled with their normal morning clients. I hurried and grabbed my normal, and then headed over to the shop. Every time I pulled up, there was a rush of pride that went through me seeing our little place sitting there, ready for the tourists and locals that came, happy that I had my own little slice of comfort. It never got old.

As I got to the door, one of our customers opened it up for me and I smiled, though I didn't recognize them. We had a multitude of regulars, strange hipsters, usually implants from San Francisco that rarely bought anything besides coffee and usually just perused the books or sat around on their laptops. I didn't mind, though. It was nice to have people in the shop and it added to the ambience when the tourists came through. They always stared at the eclectic array of local decoration in human form as if they were standing outside the gates of the zoo watching the zebras in their less than natural habitat.

I hurried through and grabbed the door with my heel so it wouldn't slam shut. To my left, on the old brown leather couch that we had shoved into a small space in the corner, was Harry, one of our regulars. He was tall and thin, his skin pale and his cheeks red. His shaggy hair folded over his forehead and he was always wearing some form or derivative of the same exact outfit. A T-shirt that the writing on was too faded to understand, either a brown, black, or blue vest, jeans, and flip-flops. He glanced up from whatever book he was reading as he sipped his coffee and gave me a nod.

I gave a half smile and nodded back, realizing

I had never really had a conversation with him even though he had been coming into the shop since... Well, as long as I could remember. He never seemed to age, even a day. He must have inherited those awesome genes that had seemed to skip my generation.

At the first line of bookshelves was another regular, Esmeralda, a middle-aged woman, only about five or six years older than me, in a broom skirt, a tank top, and a scarf with cats printed on it. Her hair, as usual, was a wired frazzled mess, barely held down by her choice in headbands that were most likely purchased several decades before.

As my eyes shifted around the room, I found Willa standing in front of the desk, leaned to the side, flipping through the pages of some old book she had picked up at a yard sale that no one would probably ever buy. As if she could sense me, she glanced up and a smile moved across her lips. "It's about damn time. Did they have to make the croissants?"

I rolled my eyes and wobbled as I crossed one leg over the other, lifting my arms out to the side, one hand holding the tray of drinks and the other the bag of croissants as I bowed to Willa. "I'm so sorry your Majesty. Had I known you had been without sustenance for all these nights, I would have hurried a little bit faster."

She chuckled, her voice high-pitched as usual, and flipped her pink hair back over her shoulder. She pulled her shoulders back and lifted her chin, rolling her hand in the air. "I forgive thee for now. You have brought my elixir of life."

We both laughed as I walked over to the counter and set the coffees down, picking hers up and handing it over to her. Whipped cream was oozing out of the hole in the lid. "Here is your fancy coffee, basically made of nothing but sugar and a few coffee beans thrown in. And here's your bag of croissants. And Happy Birthday best friend."

Willa pushed her green framed glasses up her nose and clapped her hands together, taking the coffee and putting it to her lips. She took a sip and rolled her eyes back, acting as if the drink it-self gave her life.

I nodded toward the coffee cups that she had pulled out. "Now, put it in your cup before we start having to charge the Café for promoting their business. How does it feel to reach the forty-year milestone?"

Willa sighed and then chirped. "Like I'm 240 years old. Young, young, young."

As I walked around the counter, glancing down at the events sheet that we had taped at the front in order to remind people when we were having signings or special readings, I could feel Willa's eyes glaring at me. Slowly I lifted my chin, raising a brow at her. "What's wrong? Did I forget something this morning? Did I forget to maybe draw on my eyebrows or something?"

Willa smiled and shook her head. "No. I just feel like you're super stressed today. What's going on?"

I chuckled and shook my head. "Nothing. I'm just tired, that's all."

That was totally a lie. I knew that she could see it. Willa had always had this amazing ability to know exactly what I was feeling at any moment. For a while I thought that maybe I had lost my ability to hide my emotions, something I had learned when I was younger, but she was the only one who could do it. Truth be told, I was stressed out. There were a ton of things to do, not to mention the surprise I had planned later for Willa. I always had a terrible time holding secrets from her, but this was important to me. Willa had always done so much for me, and we had known each other for almost all of our lives. I really had the chance to do something for her that she didn't see coming and that night, under the guise of a movie night, I was planning a little surprise party for her.

I had already turned forty, and Willa had thrown a big party for me, mostly filled with people from the shop, people I really didn't know. It was my turn to do something for her and I knew she would love it. I just had to get through the day without letting on to the secret. Willa also had a really great way of getting things out of me, and by the time I was done telling her all of my secrets, I didn't even realize that she coaxed them out of me. In fact, I could barely even think back and pinpoint the moment that she did it. But her birthday surprise was going to stay a surprise. I was determined, and when I set my mind to something, I was pretty damn stubborn about it.

I cleared my throat, glancing up as someone walked in the door. Willa perked and smiled at the new guest who gave off kind of an awkward air. There were usually two types of people that came into the shop. There were those that were tourists and wanted to talk to the owners, wanted to look all around the shop, and were usually relatively loud. Then there were the loners, the ones who came in with their skinny jeans rolled at the bottom, a journal of some sort under their arm, and a look as if they just wanted to be left alone. Those were my favorite people. I wasn't the more social one of the group. Willa, she loved the boisterous ones. She looked at them how they looked at the hipsters. I couldn't help but chuckle every time she held a conversation with a tourist. It was as if she had never talked to a human being before. She was fascinated.

"Have we had many people in this morning?"

Willa swallowed her bite of chocolate croissant and shook her head. "Not yet. I'm sure we'll be slammed this weekend though. It's the Pescadero Arts and Fun Festival. So, most likely they'll all be excited to look around the festival for the first day or two and then decide to drive out here and see the ocean and the scenery."

I wrinkled my nose. "Last year was so annoying. The tourists were extra loud and vivacious. I half expected for somebody to walk through the door playing a banjo at one point."

"Yeah, but we made bank, we got rid of all those books that had been sitting on the shelf forever."

I pointed at Willa. "Yes, I remember that. You were on fire. It was like every person that came through the door, you knew exactly what book to sell them. It was magical and I rarely had to talk to anybody, which made it all the more worth it to me."

Willa grunted, her mouth full of croissant, her hands brushing together as she hurried around the counter and leaned down, pulling out a flyer. It wasn't something she had printed on the computer though. It was a slightly odd compilation of what looked to be cut out beach balls, a hand drawn ocean scene, with the words "Welcome! Come relax, enjoy a coffee, read a book, and stare at the ocean at the Lustrous Bean!"

"I made this to put on the door this weekend. You know, to catch people's eye."

I gave her a half smile and chuckled as one of the glued-on beach balls fluttered off to the ground where it would probably be stuck to our tiled floors for the next five years. She shrugged, setting it carefully down on the counter. "I've been working on my art skills, but alas, I don't think it's my calling. Nor do I think the writing portion of it is either. Maybe if I laminated..."

I stared at her for a moment and then burst into laughter. "I don't know where your parents grew you, or what garden they plucked you from, but you are the weirdest person I have ever met."

She grinned, nodding her head. "That's why we're best friends. Weird attracts weird."

I glanced up at our regulars milling about the place. "We might as well join together, otherwise things would get really boring."

As much as I liked boring, I didn't know what I would've done through the years without Willa.

Keep Reading!
Grab Your Copy Now!

ABOUT THE AUTHOR

Melinda Chase is an emerging author of
Paranormal Women's Fiction.

Over forty years young, Melinda loves writing
tales that prove life—romance—and 'happily-
ever-afters'—*do exist* beyond your twenties!

Her debut Series, *Midlife Mayhem* is a snarky,
hilarious, romantic adventure, sure to please fans
of traditional paranormal romance and cozy
paranormal mysteries!

Join her newsletter at her website:
https://melindachasebooks.com/

Made in the USA
Coppell, TX
25 August 2021

61219538R00146